"*E*ven in the abyss of despair, her voice was a beacon, *guiding him through the storm,*

*her spirit a lighthouse to his drifting heart.*"

JANNIK PETTERSON

# Beyond the Crash

By Jannik Petterson

# Prologue

They were finally in the air, heading back from their idyllic honeymoon in Bora Bora. Dave and Rose had cherished every moment of their time there, but now, due to several delays, their return flight was delayed by 8 hours. Despite the extended wait, Dave looked at Rose with joy and love in his eyes, and she returned his gaze with her own warm, brown eyes.

As the captain announced the fasten seatbelt light, indicating their departure, he also mentioned an unforeseen storm ahead. Dave tried to reassure Rose, joking that the flight would be a "fun and bumpy ride home." However, as the plane ventured deeper into the storm, the turbulence grew stronger, feeling like driving down a rough dirt road at high speeds.

The plane began to drop in altitude, causing a sensation of weightlessness. Rose gripped Dave's hand tightly as they both felt the intensity of the situation. They were unable to speak, overwhelmed by the free fall of the plane. Rose wanted to scream, but only tears escaped her eyes. In that terrifying moment, Dave held onto Rose, promising to never let go, as if trying to anchor them both in the midst of chaos.

Suddenly, the plane crashed into the South Pacific Ocean,

just 20 minutes after takeoff. The impact was devastating, leading to the loss of many lives and leaving those who survived in a state of shock and disbelief. Among the wreckage and chaos, Dave awoke, disoriented and searching for Rose. He called out for her, his voice desperate and filled with fear.

As Dave swam through the debris and bodies of passengers, he realized the gravity of the situation. Hours passed as he searched, feeling broken and defeated. Eventually, overcome by exhaustion and his injuries, Dave had no choice but to give up his search. As he felt the cold water rushing over him, he resigned himself to what he believed was the end.

# Chapter One

It all began in late April of 1987, in a small, cramped house in southern Missouri. Dave was born to Dee and Jack, a mechanic who managed a modest living fixing cars. Jack's income was decent, but the growing inflation of the 1980s made it increasingly difficult for the family to stretch their dollars. Life was a constant struggle to keep up with bills and everyday expenses.

Jack was a skilled mechanic but plagued by a drinking problem, often driving home intoxicated. Dave, even at a young age, dreaded these car rides, silently praying that his mother would be the one to pick him up from school instead. He knew the dangers, even if he couldn't articulate them.

One fateful evening in late August, Jack was driving back from a neighboring town where he'd gone to help a friend with a car restoration—a hobby that brought him fleeting moments of joy in his otherwise stress-laden life. He cherished these rare escapes, a brief respite where his hands, stained with grease and his mind focused on the intricate mechanics, could forget the daily grind. It was a route he had navigated countless times, a path as familiar as the lines etched deeply in his weary face. But this night was hauntingly different.

His truck, an old Ford he had kept alive through a

combination of sheer will and mechanical prowess, seemed to have a life of its own as it tragically veered off the road. Perhaps it was a slick spot on the asphalt, or maybe just a moment's distraction at the wrong time but deep down everyone knew that the culprit was the alcohol that had become too frequent a companion in coping with the stresses of his life. Whatever the cause, the outcome was catastrophic. The truck smashed into a gnarled oak tree, the impact echoing through the silent night like a somber tolling bell.

Jack died at the scene, alone. The old Ford, his loyal companion and a testament to years of careful maintenance and repair, was now just a mangled heap of metal. The collision not only shattered the truck but also the quiet hopes and private dreams Jack harbored within him. Dreams of one day leaving his stressful life behind, of maybe opening his own restoration shop where the smell of oil and old leather would welcome him every morning instead of the cold, impersonal buzz of alarm clocks.

In the twisted wreckage, scattered among the shards of glass and splintered wood, lay the remnants of a man who had lived a life full of unspoken words and unfinished projects. The steering wheel, now cruelly bent, had been gripped by hands that once held his newborn son, hands that promised to build a better future—a future cruelly ripped away on a lonely stretch of road under the indifferent gaze of the moon.

As the night wore on, the scene remained undisturbed except for the occasional flicker of a firefly or the distant howl of a coyote. It was a solemn reminder of how fleeting life could be, of how quickly dreams could dissolve into the ether, leaving behind nothing but memories and the echoes of a life once lived.

The impact on Dave's family was catastrophic. Dee, already fragile from years of coping with her husband's addiction and the precarious finances, fell apart. Her grief was a clear, living thing that filled the house with moans and cries, especially at night when the loss became unbearable. Dave, only a child, felt his world implode. He would sit outside his mother's door, listening to her sobs, feeling helpless and abandoned in his own grief.

In the weeks that followed, the situation at home deteriorated. Dee, lost in her despair, hardly noticed as bills piled up and food became scarce. Dave missed more and more days at school, his own distress manifesting in silent, tearful withdrawals from the world.

Child Protective Services were eventually alerted by the school. One gloomy afternoon, they arrived with the sheriff, a knock at the door echoing like a thunderclap in the quiet misery of their home. Dee, a shadow of herself, answered the door to find the Sheriff and social services on her porch. Despite her protests, they insisted on entering, a court order in hand to check on Dave's wellbeing.

Inside, the house was a reflection of Dee's state of mind—neglected, chaotic, a shrine to better times now past. Dave hid under his bed, the sounds of the officials' thorough search a dull roar in his ears. After what felt like an eternity, they left, their faces grim, notes taken, and decisions unspoken. Dee was too deep in her grief to comprehend the ramifications.

Days later, without any relatives willing to intervene, Dave was removed from his home. The last image he had of his mother was her crumpled form by the window, a figure consumed by loss. In foster care, Dave was shuffled between homes, each move eroding his hope of returning to his mother. He wrote letters to Dee, filled with words of longing and confusion, but replies came infrequently, each more disjointed than the last.

One particularly cold evening, as Dave sat in the foster home living room, a sheriff arrived— the same one who had been there the day he was taken away. With a heavy heart, the sheriff delivered the news: Dee had ended her own life, overwhelmed by grief and loneliness. She had been found with Dave's last letter clutched to her chest, a final connection to her son. Her death was a solitary act of despair, a knife found by her side, the fatal wound a stark testament to her unbearable pain.

At her funeral, Dave stood apart, the reality of his situation settling in like a cold fog. His mother had left him, first to her grief, then to death. Anger and sorrow warred within him, each emotion grappling for dominance.

In the aftermath, Dave was adopted by a kind couple who had followed his story. They offered him stability and a chance at a new life, but the shadows of his past haunted him. His adoptive parents, gentle and patient, worked to breach the walls he had built around his heart.

Years passed, and Dave's life slowly transformed. He channeled his pain into academics and sports, excelling in school and becoming a star basketball player. His last letter from Dee, discovered among her belongings, was a catalyst for change. She had scribbled a message at the bottom: "I tried, I'll always be with you." These words, filled with love and regret, propelled Dave forward, determined to live a life that would make his parents proud.

Dave's transition into adulthood was shaped by an unyielding determination to redefine his life's trajectory from one of sorrow to success. His adoptive parents supported him, providing a stable home environment and nurturing his academic ambitions. Despite their care, Dave struggled to fully embrace them as his own family. The shadow of his past, marked by the tragic loss of his biological parents, loomed large, creating a barrier he found difficult to overcome. Although grateful for their support, he couldn't shake the feeling of disconnection, a silent reminder that they were not truly his.

He excelled in high school, both academically and as a star

athlete in basketball, which had become his refuge. His skills on the court could have led to athletic scholarships, but his interest lay in the realm of business—a field where he believed he could gain control over his future and escape the lingering shadows of his past losses.

After graduating high school, Dave enrolled in a prestigious business school, determined not just to survive his studies but to excel. He immersed himself in the complexities of business theories, financial models, and strategic management. His intensity and dedication caught the attention of his professors, one of whom suggested he pursue a Doctorate in Business Administration. Energized by this guidance, Dave secured his bachelor's degree with honors and immediately enrolled in the doctoral program, focusing his dissertation on the strategic development of luxury markets.

During his doctoral studies, he interned at several high-end companies, gaining invaluable firsthand experience in the luxury goods sector. This not only provided him with industry contacts but also with practical knowledge that would prove crucial in his later career.

After earning his doctorate, Dave quickly climbed the corporate ladder at a renowned luxury goods firm. His innovative ideas and sharp business knowledge set him apart. Yet, despite his rapid ascent and the success it brought, he felt unfulfilled. The corporate world offered prestige and financial security, but Dave wanted something more personal and impactful.

Motivated by an entrepreneurial spirit and a desire to create something of his own, Dave left his corporate position to start his own business. He invested his savings and secured loans to open his first jewelry store, blending exquisite craftsmanship with unique designs aimed at the high-end custom jewelry market. His business skills and relentless work ethic ensured the store's success from the outset.

Emboldened by this initial success, Dave expanded his business. He strategically located each new store in luxury shopping districts of major cities around the world, from New York to Paris, Tokyo to Dubai. His brand became synonymous with exclusivity and elegance, and his customer-centric approach converted first-time buyers into lifelong clients.

As his empire grew, so did his reputation. Known not just for his luxurious products, Dave was also respected for his business integrity and goodwill. He supported various charities and provided scholarships for business students, reflecting his own academic journey.

By the time he opened his 28th store, Dave had not only built a global jewelry empire but had also transformed his identity from the orphaned boy in Missouri to a titan of the jewelry industry. Despite his wealth and acclaim, he remained grounded, often reflecting on his journey from the depths of his youth to the heights of his business success.

Each store opening was not just a business achievement but a milestone in his personal growth and healing. His legacy was not only in the luxury items his company crafted but in the hope and resilience his life story inspired in others. His doctoral thesis, once an academic exercise, had become a blueprint for his career—a career that was as much about building personal connections as it was about building a business.

# Chapter Two

Dave now has everything he ever wanted. He lives in a 13,000 square foot house with a beautiful view out in the middle of nowhere, the countryside. Dave drives his dream car to work every morning, a 1964 Ferrari 275 p mint condition. Dave loved his new life, what more could he want? Dave had all the money, fame and glory, everything he ever wanted. He wanted to be somebody and now was, but who he truly was, is something Dave asked himself often. Dave would often think to himself, "Who am I?" but, Dave had a tough time answering that question. Is it the constant fear of losing a loved one? Or because most of his life Dave would do wrong for the right reasons and his voids are filled with guilt?

Time continued to speed up. Months felt like days and years as months but somehow days felt as an eternity. Most of his life, time was Dave's enemy. He wished he had more time with his father who spent most of his time at the liquor store and cut his life short. He misses the good times he had with his mother Dee, the time before everything started to fall apart. Dave spent most of his time at work, he kept his mind busy daily looking to expand, to grow his business. Dave had stores all over the world. He had stores throughout the United States, Spain, Italy, and other countries.

Traveling had become second nature to Dave. He thrived on the thrill of exploring new places, which was why he had strategically spread his jewelry stores across the globe. Dave was determined not to fall into the monotonous routine that seemed to ensnare so many others. However, despite his outward success and charm, Dave harbored a deep-seated insecurity.

In his stores, Dave was a sensation. His presence alone drew in high-rolling customers, and together, they would revel in the excitement of the jewelry and the experience. Dave's charisma and salesmanship were unmatched, but deep down, he felt like he was deceiving his customers. Even though he never sold counterfeit goods or misled anyone, he couldn't shake the feeling that his likability was a façade.

Dave's ability to connect with people was unparalleled. He could navigate any social situation with ease, always knowing the right thing to say. He felt like he was constantly playing a role, the puppet master pulling the strings to keep everyone around him happy and content. It was a heavy burden to bear, and while Dave had learned to manage it, he often wished he could be more authentic.

Despite his misgivings, Dave realized that his ability to influence others could be a powerful tool. He began to use it to his advantage, not to manipulate, but to ensure that everyone around him was taken care of. In business, Dave was unstoppable. His persuasive skills allowed him to close any deal, getting exactly what he wanted while ensuring that others felt satisfied with the outcome.

Some might view Dave's actions as manipulative, but to him, it was simply using his talents to their fullest potential. He genuinely cared for those in his life and used his influence to benefit them. However, despite his outward success, Dave couldn't shake the feeling that he was living a lie, constantly questioning his true intentions and longing for a sense of authenticity.

Dave's frequent visits to Paris, France, became a refuge from the solitude that plagued him at home. He was drawn to the vibrant streets, the rich history, and the stunning architecture that seemed to whisper tales of the past. In Paris, Dave found solace in the hustle and bustle of the city, immersing himself in its culture and beauty.

A typical day for Dave in Paris often began at one of the many auctions he frequented, searching for unique treasures to add to his collection. These auctions were not just about business for Dave; they were a way for him to connect with the history and artistry of each piece he acquired. After hours of bidding and negotiating, Dave would retreat to a nearby street vendor for a simple meal of French fries and an apple galette. With his food in hand, he would find a bench overlooking the Eiffel Tower, which, as dusk settled, would begin to sparkle with a golden glow. This nightly spectacle never failed to captivate Dave, who would often sit for hours, lost in thought, as he watched the tower light up the Parisian sky.

Despite the allure of Paris, Dave's return to his hotel room marked a shift in his demeanor. Alone in his room, he would find himself consumed by the weight of his thoughts and the guilt that seemed to constantly hover over him. To numb these feelings, Dave would often turn to the mini bar, seeking temporary relief from the turmoil within.

Dave's restlessness extended beyond his travels; it was a constant presence in his life. At home, he felt adrift, lost in a sea of loneliness. While he had many friends, they were the kind that came with fame and fortune, offering superficial connections that did little to ease his solitude. Dave's decision to travel extensively was a conscious effort to avoid sinking into a darkness from which he feared he would never emerge.

Part of Dave's struggle stemmed from his complex relationship with love. He questioned the authenticity of his feelings, wondering how he could love another when he had yet to learn to love himself. The loss of his mother had left a void in his heart, a void that seemed to swallow any capacity for genuine affection. While he had experienced love in its various forms, Dave believed that true love eluded him, a distant memory from a time long past.

As Dave navigated the complexities of his emotions, he found himself grappling with the concept of love and its significance in his life. The word "love" had lost its meaning, reduced to a mere symbol of affection that failed to capture the depth of his emotions. Despite his reservations, Dave longed for a love that transcended words, a love that could fill the void left by his mother's absence.

One late evening Dave found himself in Madrid, Spain, attending a captivating auction. The room was filled with exquisite pieces, each holding a story of its own. Dave bid and won many treasures that night, but one piece, in particular, caught his eye—the Birkin Bag, a stunning creation adorned with over four thousand rose gold diamonds set in platinum. It was a piece he had been searching for, and he knew he had to have it. After securing the bag for an astonishing nine hundred and seventy thousand dollars, Dave returned to his hotel room, eager to admire his new acquisition.

However, as he unpacked his winnings, he realized the Birkin Bag was missing. Panic set in as Dave frantically searched through his belongings. He must have left it at the auction house. Without a moment to lose, Dave rushed back to the building, only to find it locked and deserted. His private flight was scheduled for early the next morning, and he knew he wouldn't be able to return before leaving. Desperation crept in as he pondered his options.

Sitting on the steps outside the darkened building, Dave weighed his choices. Should he reschedule his flight and risk missing other important auctions, or should he leave and come back for the bag? The thought of losing the bag haunted him.

Determined to find it, Dave decided he would retrace his steps back to the hotel, hoping against hope that he would find it along the way. His mind raced with questions and doubts.

But right as he stood up to leave, a light flickered on at the end of the hallway, catching Dave's attention. He approached the glass doors, knocking vigorously in the hopes of finding someone inside. After what seemed like an eternity, he gave up, assuming it was just a motion light. Just as Dave turned around to walk away, he heard the distinct sound of a lock unlatching.

Rushing back to the door, Dave was greeted by a stunning woman. Her beauty was unlike anything he had ever seen, and he felt a rush of nerves and excitement. His heart pounded in his chest as he struggled to speak. Finally finding his voice, he explained his predicament, telling her about the missing Birkin Bag.

The woman could see the urgency in Dave's eyes and invited him inside. As they talked, Dave realized that he hadn't even asked for her name. "I'm Rose," she said, and Dave introduced himself as well. Rose noticed the logo on Dave's shirt and asked, "Dave Clark?"

Clark was a name Dave had chosen for himself when he was searching for a business name, which he would later adopt as his last name. "Yes, I am Dave Clark," he replied. Rose, like many others in the jewelry business around the world, had heard the name Dave Clark. She felt as if she were in the presence of a celebrity, starstruck but unwilling to show it. "This way, Mr. Clark," Rose directed Dave, pointing down the dark hallway where the vault was located.

Inside the vault, Dave laid eyes on the Birkin Bag, its diamonds shimmering in the bright lighting. Rose handed the bag to Dave, explaining its history. "Who is she?" Dave wondered as they left the vault. Neither Dave nor Rose spoke a word as they made their way back to the exit. Dave walked out holding his wrapped-up bag, thanking Rose for allowing him to retrieve it. They bid each other good night, and as Dave walked away, he felt an odd sense of regret. "Why didn't I speak with her more?" he thought. Turning back, he started walking toward the building, but Rose had already left. Dave returned to his room, thoughts of Rose lingering in his mind.

The next morning, the luggage service picked up Dave's belongings as usual, delivering them cleaned and ready for his next destination. An armored truck with three guards collected the items he had purchased the night before, transporting them to the airport to be delivered to Dave's vault in the States. Dave's limo arrived to take him to the airport, where his private jet awaited, fueled and ready. Usually eager for his next auction, this time was different. He couldn't shake thoughts of Rose from his mind, even as he tried to focus on his trip to Italy.

As Dave's jet approached its destination, he decided to review the items he planned to bid on. While scrolling through the website, he stumbled upon a link to the auction company he had visited the day before in Spain. There, he saw her: Rose, the owner of the auction company. Rose had recently inherited several locations around Europe and the United States. Dave was captivated by her eyes, lost in that moment, in her picture. He knew he had to see her again. He couldn't get her beautiful brown eyes out of his mind, so rich and soft. During his next auction, all he could think about was Rose. She was all he wanted to think about.

That day, Dave decided not to bid on any items. He only wanted to return to Spain. He needed to see her again, not just to be in her presence, but to feel those feelings once more —the joy, the excitement, the feelings Dave thought he had lost many years ago. After the auction, Dave headed straight back to the airport. He was going back to Spain, determined to ask her to dinner without any hesitation for the first time.

Upon landing in Spain, Dave's limo was waiting for him at the terminal, thanks to the pilots who had called ahead. Dave rushed to the limo, and they headed straight to the auction house owned by Rose. As they left the airport, the driver had to take a detour due to a car accident ahead. As they got closer, they stopped at a red light, just two blocks from the auction house. Dave had just finished a phone call. After hanging up, he looked out the window and saw her—Rose, more beautiful than ever.

Dave yelled for the driver to stop. The driver started to slow down, and Dave jumped out of the limo before it came to a complete stop. He walked toward Rose, his mind racing. As he got closer, just as he was about to speak, he saw her hug and kiss another man. Dave felt like he'd been hit in the chest with a baseball bat. He couldn't breathe, his body felt like it was trying to escape. Crushed and speechless, he hid behind a telephone booth and watched Rose until they left. Later that evening, Dave went back to the airport, not to fly to his next auction, but to go back home.

Midflight, caught in a whirlwind of nostalgia, Dave impulsively asked the pilot to alter their course and head toward Missouri, the state of his childhood memories. Upon landing, he found himself seated in the plush interior of a limousine, directing the driver toward the familiar streets of his old neighborhood. Steering toward the house where he had lived with his parents, it had been years since he was taken away.

As the limousine glided through the neighborhood, bathed in the golden hue of the afternoon sun, the sight of the familiar houses stirred a complex mix of emotions. The homes, with their weathered brown roofs and peeling paint, lined the street just as they had decades ago. These were the roofs under which he had once found safety and happiness, each one echoing fragments of his childhood laughter and days spent playing until dusk.

Approaching his childhood home, the luxury of the limousine felt starkly out of place against the modesty of the small, weathered house. While everything appeared remarkably unchanged—the same cracked walkway leading up to the front porch, the same rusty mailbox tilting slightly at the corner—Dave knew the warm embrace of home he longed for might be elusive. The comfort and warmth that had once filled these spaces were tied to times and people long past, and he braced himself for the dissonance between his cherished memories and the present reality.

The house itself stood stoic, its facade a testament to the years it had witnessed. It looked smaller now, diminished somehow by the years of growth and change that Dave had experienced since his departure. Yet, the emotional gravity of the place pulled at him, a tangible reminder of the life he had once known.

Dave's eyes teared up, his heart raced, and he couldn't breathe. "Don't stop, keep going," he told the driver. Dave couldn't look at the house, afraid of the memories, especially his mother Dee's death. Despite this, all he could think about was Rose, the comfort she brought.

He stayed in a hotel that night to avoid going home. The mini-bar wasn't enough, so he tried to order more alcohol, but room service had finished for the night. Dave decided to go out and get more alcohol to drink away his feelings, as he usually did.

Dave called a cab to take him to the store, but it never showed up, so he started to walk. After fifteen minutes of walking, Dave started to feel an overwhelming fullness in his chest. It was a pain unlike any he had ever felt before. Breathing became impossible; he was sweating yet freezing at the same time. Dave needed to sit down, thinking he just needed a minute, but that wasn't it. As he staggered toward a couple of milk crates stacked two high to sit on, the pressure in his chest became so intense that he couldn't even force a breath. He grew lightheaded and then fainted. Dave had a heart attack that night, and it would take some time for anyone to find him.

# Chapter Three

It was cold and dark, then the rain started. Dave laid in the street, all alone, no one around to help him. He laid there for quite some time until a homeless person found him. The homeless person began CPR as soon as he noticed Dave had stopped breathing. "Can you hear me?" the homeless person yelled as he gave chest compressions. "Help! Anyone!" he screamed as loud as he could until two more passersby came running up to help. One called 911, and the other took over CPR as he was certified.

Beep...Beep...Beep...Beep, is all he could hear for what seemed like forever. Dave slowly started to open his eyes, still very confused. "Where am I?" Dave thought as he began to see more clearly. After several minutes, he realized that he was in a hospital. "Hello?" he started to say with his scratchy voice due to being intubated at the scene by paramedics. "Is anyone there?" but no one could hear him. He noticed a button on the side of the bed that looked like a call button, so he pressed it. Not long after pressing the button, a nurse came in and started checking his vital signs with excitement due to Dave waking up. Everything looked great to the nurse, she turned to Dave and explained that he had been in the hospital for several days due to a heart attack. Dave was confused, "what do you mean several days?" he asked as his heart rate started to climb.

The nurse couldn't give Dave much information as the Doctor would be coming in soon to explain everything. Dave was still so confused, "Why can't I remember anything?" and "how would I not remember the last several days?" He felt as if he was living in a nightmare with no answers. Moments later, the Doctor knocked on the door as he entered the room. "Hello Dave!" the Doctor said loudly with a big smile on his face, "We didn't know if you would wake up again." At this point, Dave was starting to get nervous, "what do you mean wake up?" "how long have I been out?" he asked the doctor. So, the doctor started to explain everything that had happened to Dave since the night of his heart attack.

When Dave collapsed, he had lost a lot of blood flow to the brain. Although he was found just in time to get his heart beating again, Dave had lost a lot of oxygen to his brain. The Doctor explained that with the lack of oxygen, Dave had fallen into a hypoxic coma for three days. He also noted that, the amount of alcohol in his body that night, could have killed him alone. Dave didn't remember that he not only drank all the drinks stocked in his mini bar at the hotel, but not long before, Dave drank all available drinks in his limo while trying to build up courage to visit his childhood home. All he could do was to lay his head back on the reclined hospital bed and turn his head towards the window so he could think.

Dave would need to stay in the hospital for several more weeks to recover as many patients that suffer from cerebral hypoxia do not survive. Yet Dave seemed mostly healthy after being in a coma for three days. All the doctors working at that hospital were surprised how well Dave was doing but he still had a long journey ahead of him. Dave needed physical therapy on his right leg as movement was limited, he also had a mild case of long-term memory loss. When Dave was asked what his birthdate was, he kept giving the wrong date later realizing it was the date of his father's birth. But overall, Dave was in decent shape.

While at the hospital, Dave attended rehab that

specialized in alcohol use disorder to help him overcome his addiction. Addiction was a word Dave had never used before when describing himself, he always thought he could stop whenever he wanted without any issues but why stop when it helps cover up the pain, the feelings of loneliness and despondency. At least that's what he always thought to justify his drinking. Dave would attend for one hour every day while he stayed in the hospital to recover.

During his last few days at the hospital, Dave started to pack his belongings and set everything together just in case he would be discharged sooner. Later that evening, there was a knock on his room door. "Come in" Dave called out and the door opened slowly, just as it did, Dave smelled a familiar scent, it was so sweet and warm. What Dave saw next, made him believe that he was dreaming, or that he may have just died and started to see angels. The room was semi-dark and Dave's eyes tried to adjust to the lights that came from the hallway into the room from behind this person and then he heard a soft voice speaking. "Hello Dave" "It's Rose, we met a little while ago in Spain".

Dave didn't know how to react, what could he say?

"Rose?" "How are you?" Dave replied, just to spark a conversation, after minutes of silence in disbelief. "I'm doing fine Dave," "I know this must be strange, strange that I am here." Dave, as always, tried to make the best of all situations and certainly this one. "Why are you here?" Dave asked Rose. Of course, this wasn't the best question he could have asked but, under the circumstances, that's the only thing that came to his mind.

Rose had only met Dave once before, a brief encounter that left a lasting impression on her. Despite the shortness of their meeting, she couldn't shake the connection she felt. When news of Dave's critical condition surfaced, her previous hesitation melted away. The thought of never seeing him again, never exploring what might have been, spurred her into action. The feelings Dave had been feeling since he met Rose were mutual.

"I'm not sure why I'm here but, I had to tell you how I feel," Rose said, her voice wavering.

Dave was at a loss for words. He felt a surge of emotions but was paralyzed by the fear of saying the wrong thing. As he looked into Rose's eyes, he realized that moments like these didn't need perfect words—they needed honesty. So, he took a deep breath and expressed how deeply he felt about her, letting his heart speak the truth.

Expressing his feelings to Rose, Dave felt relieved now that she knew how he felt about her. They spent the rest of the evening together, talking and laughing over a hot cup of tea and Jell-O from the hospital cafeteria. They talked all night until sunrise when the doctor came in to discharge Dave.

The doctor explained that once he returned home, Dave should follow up with his primary doctor and continue with physical therapy for his leg. He was given recommendations and referrals for his drinking problem, close to his home. Dave signed out and left the hospital.

Instead of going home, Dave checked into a nearby hotel. He needed a long, hot shower to recoup. Rose also had a room at the same hotel, and they had dinner plans later that evening. After his shower, Dave sat at the end of his bed, staring at his reflection on the TV screen until there was a knock on the door. It was the hotel staff delivering his freshly cleaned suit.

Dave got ready for his dinner date, wearing his custom-fit Zegna suit and dress shoes. He didn't like ties, so he wore just his white undershirt. As he arrived at the restaurant, he noticed Rose was already there, sitting at a table in the center of the dining room.

Rose was the most beautiful soul in the restaurant, her hair as golden as the sun. Every time Dave saw her, his heart raced, his legs weakened, and she was all he could focus on. They spent hours together, not caring about the time, only about each other.

But the evening had to come to an end.

The next morning, both Dave and Rose had to say their goodbyes. Dave had to fly back home to get back to work. Rose had meetings for her auction company. But it wouldn't be long before Dave would return to Spain on a business trip to visit Rose.

Neither Dave nor Rose could focus on work, only on each other. Dave would spend days at a time with Rose at her home. After he returned home to the states, Rose would randomly surprise him. Every time, he would stop what he was doing, and together they would take off.

A year passed since Dave met Rose, yet he still got butterflies in his stomach every time he saw her. He couldn't stand that they lived so far apart; he wanted to be closer. His feelings grew so strong that he didn't understand how to deal with them. Would he move to Spain, or would he ask Rose to move to the States? How could he ask her to do that? Dave didn't know what to do, until a few days later. He decided to move to Spain and turn his store there into the home office of his company.

Before finalizing his decision, Dave wanted to discuss it with Rose first, ensuring she was on board. He took her to her favorite restaurant and, after they ate, he asked, "Rose, how would you feel about me moving here, to Spain? I have an apartment above my store, and I can live there." Rose remained quiet, spinning her empty wine glass on the table, lost in thought. Finally, she looked up and said, "No."

Dave felt a tightness in his chest, his breathing heavy. "Oh," he replied. But before he could say more, Rose stopped him. She clarified that she didn't mean "no" to moving to Spain. Instead, she didn't want him moving into the apartment; she wanted them to live together.

Rose expressed that the location didn't matter to her; what mattered was being with Dave. His face lit up, brimming with excitement. He told her to choose a place anywhere in the world, and he would make it their home, a place to start their life together. However, Rose noticed his excitement waning, replaced by what seemed like sadness, suggesting something weighed on his mind.

Dave had suffered memory loss after his heart attack, forgetting about the man he had seen with Rose. "Dave, what's wrong?" Rose asked, reaching for his hand. Dave hesitated, not wanting to ask about the man and risk their relationship but he had to know.

"Before my heart attack, I was coming to see you, Rose," he explained. "I couldn't stop thinking of you, but I hid once I saw you two, you and another man." Rose, confused, assured him she hadn't been with anyone else for years. Uncomfortable with the topic, Dave tried to avoid discussing it further.

Rose asked Dave to describe the man, triggering her memory. She clarified, "Dave, this wasn't anyone I was seeing; it was a French client of mine. We met for lunch to go over some plans." Relieved, Dave felt tension ease between them, though it lingered.

Leaving the restaurant, they walked in silence, the moonlight guiding them. As their fingers intertwined, Rose said, "We can live in the U.S." She explained she had less to give up, being able to work from anywhere, and they could still visit Spain regularly. They decided Rose would move in with him.

Over the next few month, they transitioned to living together in Dave's home. Even now, they couldn't stand to be apart, doing everything together. Dave treated Rose like royalty, their love was strong, caring, and faithful. They had all they ever wanted: each other.

Everything seemed like a fairytale; nothing could stop Dave with Rose by his side. He grew his 28 stores into 40 the year after Rose moved in with him. Rose started working with Dave on certain projects as she would have time away from her auction business. Together, they built the most luxurious jewelry company with stores all around. Not only were they true lovers, but they also became the best partners.

As the next few years drifted by, Dave knew that he wanted to grow old with Rose. His love for her was stronger now than ever before, so he decided it was time to propose to her. But how? Dave had never learned how to be romantic, so he always chose to be himself. Most of his life, that worked out great for him, but he knew that he needed to do more for Rose.

Dave spent months planning the proposal until the day he felt ready; the time was right. Dave was heading to Paris for an auction. Rose planned on meeting him that day in Paris as she was flying in from Spain. Together, they stayed at the auction until it closed, bidding on many beautiful items, some for the stores and some Dave wanted Rose to have.

There was one item that Dave had purchased that Rose didn't know about. Before the auction started, Dave made a cash offer on the flawless oval diamond ring that Rose adored when she saw it advertised several days prior. The starting bid for the ring started at one hundred thousand euros but projected to reach over nine hundred thousand. Dave made a cash offer of 1.2 million euros and the seller accepted.

After the auction, Dave did as usual, but this time he had Rose with him. It was two orders of French fries and two apple galettes. They made their way towards the Eiffel Tower and sat on the same bench that Dave would always go to after a long day at the auction. After they finished eating, there was a little more time than usual before the tower would start sparkling its lights. Dave and Rose took a walk around the tower and enjoyed its beauty. Several moments later, the tower started to sparkle; it was dark and warm out but with a gentle cool breeze. The sky was lit up with what seemed like a billion stars. It was perfect.

Dave and Rose took several steps back to enjoy the beauty of the sparkling lights on the tower while looking straight up. Dave stood behind Rose with his arms wrapped around her, holding her tight until he stepped back. Rose turned around, but Dave wasn't there, until she looked down. Rose started breathing heavily and quickly; her heart could be heard beating in her ears, tears forcing themselves out, with no holding back. Dave was on one knee with a black ring box in his hand.

"Rose, when I'm with you, the world around me stops, all my problems fade away, and my days are brighter," Dave said. Still, while on one knee, Dave continued, "Before I met you, I feared commitment, I didn't know what love felt like, but you changed everything, you reset my life for the absolute better." At this point, Rose was crying and dropped to her knees in front of Dave with so much joy and love in her eyes. Dave then opened the ring box that held the oval diamond ring and continued. "Rose, I can't imagine a single day without you; you are a part of my heart and soul," and right as the Eiffel Tower was fully covered in the golden hue from the lights, he asked, "Rose, will you marry me?" Rose fell into Dave's arms and cried, "YES, Dave! YES!"

This day was the happiest day in both of their lives.

# Chapter Four

Rose couldn't wait to call all her family in Spain to tell them the good news. She was so happy; nothing would bring her down. Dave, on the other hand, didn't have anyone to call. Since he cut off all contact with his adoptive family many years ago, it had just been him until he met Rose. Dave wasn't happy about his decision since he was always treated with love and respect; he just couldn't give it in return. He felt it was easier to cut them out of his life rather than standing up to his feelings. It was the easy way out.

A few days after Dave proposed, they both returned home to the U.S.

Dave wanted to do something special for Rose. While she was on a late-night conference call, he prepared for a full night of intimacy. He had a tough time planning the night; this was a first-time experience for him. He took one step at a time, one room at a time. First, Dave lit candles throughout every room. Rose petals, that he picked himself from his garden that day, led the way to the bathroom where he drew up a bath, steaming and bubbly. All lights in the home were dimmed. Salt rock lamps six feet tall were lit in all corners of the home; the atmosphere was warm and relaxing.

Once Rose finished her call, she opened the door that led from her office to the living room and was surprised. The room was dark but bright enough to see from the warm lighting of the lamps and all the candlelight. Rose followed the rose petal-paved way throughout the home leading to the bathroom. Once at the end of the rose trail, Rose found Dave with a bottle of Dom Perignon champagne and a warm bathroom with a filled tub of hot soapy water.

While Dave filled two glasses of champagne, Rose changed into her silk robe behind her shoji screen. She walked out from behind her screen and dropped her robe right as she was stepping into the bathtub, one foot at a time. As she sat back and relaxed, Dave served her the champagne. After, Dave as well changed into his robe only to take it off right after so he could join Rose in the tub. Rose slid herself between his legs while resting her back against his chest with her head on his right shoulder.

Together, Dave and Rose lounged in the tub, champagne in hand, for hours. The water stayed warm; time irrelevant. After, they enjoyed a dinner Dave had prepared, him still in his robe as he set the table and finished side dishes before Rose emerged from her dressing room. He hurried to have everything ready and perfect for her.

When Rose entered, the candlelit room took her breath away. The table was set with fine China and crystal glasses. Dave pulled out her chair and poured her wine. He lifted the dish cover, and the aromas enveloped her. "This looks and smells amazing, Dave," she said.

That night was special. Despite Dave's doctor's advice not to drink, and his attendance at AA meetings, they indulged. It was all about Rose. They finished dinner and went to bed, but the night didn't end there. Their love was rough yet gentle, beautiful, and passionate. They fell asleep in each other's arms.

Over the next months, they planned their wedding. There was much to do, with guests coming from around the world.

They stepped back from work, letting their teams handle things, focusing on themselves and the wedding. They attended auctions but did less selling and administrative work.

Before the wedding, Dave and Rose decided to sell his home. They planned to buy or build a home together. The home was put on the market, and they started deciding on what to do. They didn't have long, as building would take up to a year.

Offers came in quickly. They were fair, but it wasn't about the money. They accepted an offer that gave them two months to move out, allowing time to decide their next step.

One evening, Dave suggested, "An island!" Rose was puzzled. Dave explained he'd read about a couple living on an island, listing several islands for sale. Rose was unsure, concerned about the potential loneliness. Dave agreed, realizing it was a silly idea.

However, Dave's interest persisted. Rose secretly researched island living, considering the pros and cons. She liked that some islands were only a short boat ride from the mainland, and with Dave's helicopter license, travel would be even faster. She didn't tell Dave, wanting to be certain.

After more research, Rose decided she was okay with island living. When she told Dave, he jumped on the bed with excitement. They started looking at islands for sale, finding many options worldwide. They selected a few to visit in person, making arrangements with the sellers.

Dave and Rose explored several islands, but none felt right. Many lacked cell signal or landlines, crucial for their work. They briefly considered a satellite phone but found it impractical. Despite the disappointing visits, Dave made each trip special, bringing a picnic basket with sandwiches, wine, roses, and a blanket for comfort. Treating each island visit like a vacation, Dave hoped to make the best of any location for Rose's sake, knowing she supported the idea only for him.

After the fifth island, Dave decided to abandon the idea of island living. He planned to discuss it with Rose later, after her business conference calls. However, during one call, Rose excitedly discovered an island in the Bahamas, Caribbean, through one of her investors. It was 350 acres, about half the size of Central Park in New York City.

"Dave, I found it!" Rose exclaimed, showing him the printout. Unsure how to respond, Dave hesitated. Should he tell her he had changed his mind? He still liked the idea but feared Rose's unhappiness.

Dave kept his thoughts to himself that day, planning to talk to Rose before making a final decision. He wanted her to be sure, not just doing it for him, but for herself as well. When they visited the island a few days later, they were both stunned by its beauty.

In the past, the island had been a resort but was now a private retreat. The owners had taken great care of it, but after the previous owner's death, it went into foreclosure. Dave and Rose could purchase it for under thirty million dollars, a fraction of its seventy-five million dollar value, which they could finance with a loan. The island included beaches, golf courses, luxury villas, and a resort, with a ten-bedroom mansion for them to live in.

Over the next few weeks, they visited the island multiple times to explore every corner. Dave planned to add more solar panels to reduce reliance on diesel generators. They decided to buy the island, but whether they would reopen it to the public or keep it private was a decision they would make after the wedding.

As they explored the island further, Dave and Rose discovered hidden coves with crystal-clear waters, perfect for snorkeling and diving. They found lush forests teeming with exotic wildlife, and secluded beaches where they could watch the sunset in peace. Each day brought new adventures and discoveries, strengthening their bond and confirming their decision to make this island their home.

As they sat on the veranda of the mansion, overlooking the azure waters, Dave took Rose's hand in his. "I can't imagine a more perfect place to spend the rest of our lives," he said, gazing into her eyes.

Rose smiled, her heart full of love for this man and excitement for their future together. "I agree," she said, leaning in to kiss him. "This island is our paradise, and I can't wait to call it home."

With their decision made, Dave and Rose began making plans for their new life on the island. They hired a team to help them renovate the mansion and update the resort facilities. As they worked together to bring their vision to life, Dave and Rose grew even closer, their love for each other deepening with each passing day.

Moving to the island was a monumental undertaking that stretched over many weeks. It was a complex process, especially considering that Dave and Rose had to coordinate the shipment of their belongings from Spain, where they had been living after selling their home in the U.S. Despite the logistical challenges and the considerable expense involved, the decision to move was one they never regretted.

The island greeted them with its pristine beauty. The air was so fresh and clean, filled with the scent of the sea. The water surrounding the island was a stunning shade of blue, so clear that they could see the ocean floor. The sound of the waves crashing against the shore and the gentle ocean breeze provided a constant, soothing backdrop to their new life.

One of Rose's favorite moments was sipping her morning coffee on the wrap-around deck, taking in the breathtaking views. Dave often joined her, wrapping his arms around her and whispering, "It's a dream come true," a sentiment that echoed her own feelings.

As the weeks passed, Dave and Rose began to settle into their new home. The mansion was almost fully furnished, and most of their belongings had arrived. They took the time to explore every building, shop, and amenity on the island. They inspected all the villas, which they planned to use as guest homes for Rose's family, some of Dave's close work friends, and any future visitors after the wedding. For other guests, they had arranged accommodation at a nearby resort, which they would cover until their return flights home.

Contractors that they had hired began flying in to start the necessary repairs and maintenance around the island. With most of their initial tasks completed, Dave and Rose took the opportunity to travel. Rose flew back to Spain for a few weeks, while Dave visited his stores and attended auctions. During this time, Dave managed to acquire five more stores, bringing his total to forty-five, with the home office still based in Spain.

Before returning to the island, Dave and Rose decided to take a detour to Paris, a city they both loved. They took a train from Barcelona to Paris, where they indulged in their favorite street food and admired the Eiffel Tower. After spending a night in the city of lights, they started their journey back to the island.

It was during this leg of their journey that Rose noticed a small photo album in Dave's hands, one she had never seen before. Dave explained that he had kept it stored in the safe at their Spain location for safekeeping. It contained all the remaining memories of his mother, a treasure trove of moments captured in photographs and mementos.

As they made their way through the airport towards the terminal, a wheel on Dave's suitcase suddenly fell off. He knelt down to fix it, inadvertently laying the album down on Rose's suitcase. When he stood up, he accidentally knocked over Rose's suitcase, causing the album to slide across the ground and letters addressed to Dee to scatter all over the floor.

Without hesitation, Rose began collecting the postcards and letters. As she handed them to Dave, she noticed that they all had the same sending and receiving addresses. It was then that she realized they were letters to and from Dave's mother, Dee Clark. She gently asked Dave about them, and he confirmed that they were indeed letters that he had written to his mother, including the final letter she had received before her tragic suicide.

Dave and Rose continued through the terminal, a heavy silence hanging between them. It felt like hours had passed without a word spoken, each lost in their thoughts. Rose couldn't shake the image of Dave's childhood from her mind, knowing the emotional turmoil it had caused him before.

She remembered the story Dave had once shared about trying to visit his childhood home, only to be overwhelmed by emotions. As they neared the plane's gate, a thought struck her, and she halted, pulling Dave out of the line with her. "Let's go visit your childhood home before heading back!" she suggested, her voice gentle but insistent. Dave hesitated, preferring to just board the plane and return home, but Rose was persistent. She believed facing his fears was essential, especially after all they had been through together. After some convincing, Dave reluctantly agreed.

Leaving the terminal, they bought tickets to Missouri, the place where Dave's past lay buried. During the twelve-hour flight, Dave wavered in his decision several times, his anxiety evident, but with Rose by his side, he felt more secure. She was his rock, his anchor in the storm of emotions that threatened to engulf him.

When they finally landed, Dave was a mix of emotions, his heart racing with anticipation and anxiety, a stark contrast to his previous visit when fear had paralyzed him.

Rose arranged for a rental car while Dave collected their luggage. They met outside the airport, and with Rose behind the wheel, they embarked on the three-hour journey to Dave's hometown. The landscape passed by in a blur, the anticipation building with each mile they traveled.

As they approached, Dave's heart raced, and Rose recognized the need to stop and calm him before proceeding. They pulled over, and Rose held his hand, offering silent support as he struggled to compose himself. After a few minutes, Dave nodded, signaling that he was ready to continue.

With Rose still driving, they approached Dave's childhood home. Memories flooded back as they neared the house. Dave, staring straight ahead, closed his eyes, took a deep breath, and then, slowly, looked out of his window.

He stared, almost transfixed, for what felt like an eternity. Rose tried to break his trance, but he remained motionless. Finally, he turned to her, tears glistening in his eyes. "I think I'm ready now," he whispered, his voice filled with a mix of emotions.

Rose led the way out of the car, Dave followed, slower, more hesitant. He reached for her hand, his touch trembling. "I want to knock," he said softly. "See if we can tour the home." His heart pounded, and his breath caught in his throat as they approached the front door. With each step, his resolve wavered.

# Chapter Five

Dave was still holding Rose's hand when the door creaked open. He tried to pull away, but her grip was firm.

A boy, about the same age Dave was when he left that home, stood in the doorway. Dave was at a loss for words. "Hi, I'm Dave," he managed to say softly. Before the boy could respond, his mother hurried to the door. Seeing Dave's discomfort, Rose stepped in, introducing themselves and explaining why they were there.

The boy's mother agreed to let them tour the house. As they walked through the living room, Dave was transported back to his childhood. Memories flooded his mind, surprisingly happy ones.

In the living room, he saw his parents laughing, and he remembered pretending to have wings as he ran through the house. In the kitchen, his father read the morning paper while his mother made breakfast. Dave walked down the hallway, past the kitchen, and hesitated at his parents' old bedroom. Unable to bring himself to enter, he thanked the homeowner and quickly walked out of the home.

He couldn't bear to enter that room, where he had often peeked through the cracked door, watching his mother in pain. He felt the same pain now but didn't know how to ask for comfort, just as he didn't know how to comfort his mother.

It was the room where his mother had committed suicide.

Back in the car, Rose was upset. "What was that, Dave?" she asked. "You stormed out after they welcomed us into their home." Dave stayed silent until a few miles before they reached the airport, where he finally apologized and explained. "I was okay until I reached my parents' old room," he said. "I felt like I was going to pass out. I had to leave, quick." Rose realized then that this was the same room where Dave's mother had ended her life.

Both fell into a heavy silence as they rode to the airport, Rose's hand seeking Dave's for comfort. They returned to the rental car parking in silence, checked their bags, and boarded the plane without a word. The flight back to their Caribbean Island home was supposed to be straightforward, but there were several delays. Exhausted and longing for their own bed, they checked into a hotel inside the airport, but rest eluded them.

When they finally boarded the next flight, the relief was great. After many hours they made it back home. "Feels good to be back," Dave exclaimed as they disembarked the water plane that shuttled them from the mainland to their island. Rose could barely muster a nod; she was drained, both mentally and physically. Dave headed off to inspect the progress of the renovations and repairs on the island, leaving Rose to retreat to their mansion for some much-needed rest.

Despite the challenges, life on the island seemed perfect upon their return. Wedding planning consumed most of their days, but they always made time for each other. Every evening, they strolled along one of the island's three beaches, watching the sun dip below the horizon. Some nights, they sat by a crackling fire, watching the moon's reflection dance on the waves. Other times, they gazed up at the star-filled sky, making wishes on shooting stars.

Their wishes were simple yet profound: to be happy. And for the most part, they were. That is until one morning when Rose was jolted awake by excruciating abdominal pain. She tried to ignore it, hoping it would pass, but the sensation only intensified. As she shifted in bed, she felt a rush of fluids. Turning on the lamp, she was overcome by numbness.

"Dave! Wake up!" Rose's panicked voice cut through the silence. Dave sprang from bed, alarmed by the urgency in her tone. "What's wrong?" he asked, his heart racing. Unable to find the words, Rose simply pointed, and Dave's heart sank. He kissed her forehead, assuring her that everything would be okay, before helping her to the bathroom to clean up and then rushing her to the emergency room.

The hours in the emergency room dragged on, filled with worry and uncertainty. Finally, a doctor emerged with news that shattered their world: Rose had suffered a miscarriage. The pain and grief were overwhelming as they clung to each other, trying to make sense of the loss.

Rose fell silent. Her mind churned with unspoken questions. What if their baby had lived? How different would their world be, filled with joy instead of this unbearable pain? She pictured their child in her arms, a life imagined but never lived. Yet outwardly, she remained stoic, her expression blank, lost in her thoughts, unable to respond to the world around her.

Rose was discharged the following morning, and together they headed to the airport for a short flight home.

Once they arrived at the airport and just before boarding the plane, Rose turned to Dave with a solemn expression. "I want to go home," she said quietly. Dave, puzzled, replied, "Rose, we are going home." "No, not to the island," she clarified, "home to Spain, with my mother, my family."

Dave was taken aback. "Oh," he murmured, tears welling up

in his eyes. "Why to Spain? You know I wouldn't be able to go with you!" They were expecting wedding planners and other vendors to visit the island to begin preparations. They needed to gather pictures and ideas to finalize the plans for their big day. At least one of them had to be on the island for these crucial meetings.

"I have to be with my mother, Dave," Rose said softly, moving closer to him. She reached up and gently cupped his face in her hands. "I love you, and I always will, but right now I need to find myself again." Dave felt a wave of panic rising inside him, but he kept his composure. "What does that mean for us?" he asked, his voice trembling. "Do I go to the island alone and plan the wedding by myself?"

Rose didn't want to call off the wedding, but she also couldn't bear to return to the island at that moment. All she wanted was to be with her mother, her family. She loved Dave deeply and didn't want to lose him, but she knew she couldn't be as happy as she once was, at least not right now.

They walked together to the ticket counter in silence. Rose asked for one ticket to Spain on the next available flight, which wouldn't depart for another three hours.

The plane that was originally meant to take them both back to the island was still waiting. Dave ended up buying his own ticket just so he could accompany Rose all the way to the boarding gate, past security. He wanted to be there in case she changed her mind, to support her no matter what. Though Rose didn't change her mind, they spent almost the entire three hours talking, trying to make sense of their feelings and their uncertain future.

"Dave, I don't want to call off the wedding. I will be back. I just need time. How long? I don't know, but I will be back." Dave smiled, looking into Rose's eyes, giving her a long, gentle kiss. As the airport attendant called passengers onto the plane, he told her he loved her. He showered her with more kisses and a warm hug, walking her to their seats using the ticket he had bought. After one final, meaningful kiss, Dave returned to the gate and watched Rose's plane ascend into the blue, sunny sky.

Alone now, Dave faced uncertainty. For a while now, Rose had been his guide. He felt lost and isolated, yet he knew he had to be strong, for himself and their future.

Returning to the island, Dave tried to resume normalcy. Eight days later, he met with the wedding planner, struggling to answer questions. How many guests? "All of them." The theme? "A happy one." The date? "Hopefully someday."

Despite daily calls with Rose, Dave's emotions unraveled. He tried to stay strong, but his feelings overwhelmed him, reminiscent of when he lost his mother, Dee. This time, he and Rose had lost their child.

Each day, he pleaded with Rose to return, needing her comfort. But Rose, battling her own demons, explained, "I can't come back yet. When we found out about the miscarriage, a part of me died too. The island was supposed to be our new beginning, but I can't be there knowing we should have another life with us. I love you; I will be back when I'm better."

Dave stood there, phone in hand, before slowly hanging up. He grabbed a $300 bottle of bourbon and a case of beer, heading to the beach. Sitting there, he drank, watching the tides, feeling a sense of peace after the first half bottle. He couldn't overdo it, so he switched to beer. As the sun set, Dave stumbled toward the water, recalling the romantic evenings with Rose.

Walking into the waves, Dave dropped the beer and submerged himself. The ocean consumed him, and he blacked out. In that moment, he felt a strange sense of relief, as if surrendering to the ocean's embrace was the only way to find comfort in his pain. The water surrounded him, washing away the tears and the ache in his heart, if only for a fleeting moment. The weight of his sorrow seemed to lessen as he drifted into unconsciousness, letting go of the world and its troubles, if only for a while.

The next morning dawned with a cold, gloomy haze settling over the beach. Rain began to fall in a gentle patter, adding to the desolate atmosphere. Dave awoke, his head barely above the water's edge, a miraculous survivor of the previous night's ordeal.

For most, such an experience would have been a wake-up call, a moment of reckoning, but not for Dave. He was different. Instead of reflecting on his near-death experience, he simply shook off the water, his thoughts drifting to the dull ache in his side, a sure sign of at least one cracked rib.

Dragging himself back to the house, each step a painful reminder of his mortality, Dave's only thought was to numb the pain. He headed straight for the kitchen, his movements slow and deliberate, pouring himself a glass of whisky. Downing two shots in quick succession, he refilled the glass, a tall, amber beacon of his intent.

With a glass in hand, Dave made his way to the bathroom, a sanctuary of sorts. He sank into the bathtub, the hot water soothing his aching body. Fully clothed, he lay there, the sound of the water mixing with the gentle rain outside, a melancholic symphony of his own making.

Meanwhile, Rose tried desperately to reach Dave, her calls echoing unanswered through the empty house. Dave, lost in his own world of pain and regret, ignored the incessant ringing of the phone. He couldn't bear for Rose to hear him like this, broken and defeated, not even over the phone.

As the day wore on, Dave continued to drink, each sip a temporary reprieve from his inner uncertainty. He was tired, tired of the endless cycle of pain and despair that seemed to define his existence. He drank until the world around him blurred and faded, until he could no longer keep his eyes open, until he fell into a deep, unconscious sleep, the whisky bottle slipping from his hand, the room spinning in a drunken whirl.

Over the next two days, there was no answer. Rose kept trying, her fingers dialing Dave's number almost automatically, hoping that this time he would pick up. But the phone just rang and rang, echoing in her ears like a taunt.

As each call went unanswered, panic tightened its grip on Rose's chest. She knew Dave was alone on the island, drowning his sorrows in alcohol. Guilt gnawed at her. She shouldn't have left him in that state, not after what they had been through, losing their baby. But she had felt she had no choice, for her own sanity, for her own survival.

Rose had believed Dave was stronger now, better able to handle his emotions. He had seemed to be coping, but deep down, she knew he had never truly stopped drinking, not since his heart attack. Alcohol had always been both his comfort and his downfall, his best friend and his worst enemy.

Despite her fears, Rose knew she had to go to the island, to check on Dave, to make sure he was okay. She quickly packed a small bag, grabbing only the essentials, leaving behind everything else, including her own worries and doubts. She ran out of her mother's house, her feet pounding the pavement as she searched for a taxi.

Luckily, there was one waiting at the curb, and Rose jumped in, giving the driver the address of the airport. As they sped towards their destination, Rose's mind raced with thoughts of Dave, of what she would find when she reached him. She prayed he was okay, that she wasn't too late.

At the airport, Rose paid the driver more than the fare, eager to be on her way. She rushed inside, her heart pounding in anticipation. At the ticket counter, she practically begged for the first flight out. The ticket clerk, a young man with tired eyes, typed furiously at his computer, checking all available flights.

After what felt like an eternity, he looked up and said, "The next flight out leaves in two hours. It'll cost you four thousand dollars and take thirty hours to get there." Rose's heart sank at the thought of the long journey ahead, but she knew she had no choice. She had to get to Dave, no matter the cost.

The clerk explained that there was an eighteen-hour layover in Newark before the final leg of the journey to the Bahamas. It was the quickest option available, he said, given the circumstances. He also mentioned that there had been a flight that left just forty-five minutes earlier that would have arrived sooner.

Without hesitation, Rose bought the ticket, ignoring the cost, ignoring the time. All that mattered was getting to Dave, making sure he was safe. She cleared security, her mind racing with thoughts of what she would say to him, how she would comfort him.

As she sat at the gate, waiting for the boarding announcement, Rose tried calling Dave one last time. The phone didn't even ring this time; it just went straight to a busy signal. Fear gripped her heart, squeezing it tight. All she wanted was to be with Dave, to hold him, to tell him everything would be okay.

Over the next nine hours of the flight to Newark, Rose was lost in thoughts, her mind racing through every possible scenario. The concern of the passengers around her was noticeable, as they glanced over, offering words of comfort and checking on her well-being. Despite their kindness, Rose remained silent, her gaze fixed on the world outside her window, where clouds drifted by in silent procession.

Upon landing in Newark, Rose's desperate attempts to reach Dave yielded only the same frustrating busy signal she had encountered since leaving Spain. Exhausted and emotionally drained, she checked into a nearby airport hotel, where she collapsed into a deep and restless sleep that lasted a staggering eleven hours.

When Rose finally awoke, the weariness had settled deep into her bones, her mind still clouded with worry, and her cheeks streaked with dried tears. The hours stretched on as she lay in bed, the weight of the unknown pressing down on her.

Eventually, she summoned the strength to make her way back to the gate for her flight home. The journey felt interminable, with each minute dragging by like an eternity. Finally, after thirty grueling hours of travel, she set foot once again on the island she called home.

To her shock, the usually vibrant island was shrouded in darkness. The familiar lights that illuminated the villas were extinguished, the grand mansion sat in shadow, and even the decorative lights that adorned the island's pathways were switched off.

Fear gripped Rose as she sprinted towards her home, her heart pounding in her chest. "Dave, I'm here! Where are you?" she called out, her voice raw with emotion, the only sound her own frantic footsteps echoing in the night.

Reaching their house, Rose found the front door wide open, inviting her into the darkness within. With a trembling step, she crossed the threshold, her voice catching in her throat as she called out for Dave one last time, only to fall to her knees in shock and disbelief.

# Chapter Six

Rose couldn't believe her eyes. Everything lay in ruins, the home they'd built together obliterated. "Dave!?" Her voice echoed through the devastation, but only silence greeted her. She pushed herself up, her heart pounding, and started to move through the wreckage. Shock held her in its grip. The windows shattered, furniture shredded, walls punctured, and pictures strewn across the floor.

In their bedroom, a trail of blood led to the bathroom. Inside, the tub overflowed, water cascading onto the floor. Rose shut off the tap, her mind racing. She called out for Dave again, her voice trembling, but there was no reply. Panic surged. She needed help, but who could she call? She made a decision; she had to return to the mainland to seek assistance. Maybe he'd left the island, she thought, as she turned to leave.

But a flicker of light caught her eye, a distant glow. "Dave!" Her voice rose, hope and fear mingling. The glow intensified, drawing her toward the nearest beach. Running blindly in the darkness, she stumbled but pressed on. She knew this path by heart. As she neared the beach, the glow transformed into a fire. Heart pounding, she sprinted forward, knowing one thing for certain: Dave was there.

When she reached the beach, relief flooded her. Dave was

indeed there, his silhouette outlined by the flames. He turned to her, his expression haunted. "Rose, I... I didn't know what to do," he stammered, tears glistening in his eyes. "I tried, I tried but failed. I failed you."

Dave had fallen apart. The new life he had built with Rose was slipping through his fingers. Past traumas gripped him tightly, stripping away his control after the loss of their unborn child and the fear of losing Rose. His once steady hands now shook with the weight of it all, drowning his sorrows in alcohol and neglecting the life they had planned together—the island preparations, the wedding arrangements, their shared dream slipping into the abyss.

Many would have walked away at this point, resigned to the seeming inevitability of their relationship's demise. But not Rose. Though she hadn't lived through Dave's past, she had glimpsed it through his eyes, and she knew he needed her now more than ever. She needed him just as much.

Dave knelt, broken, his tears flowing uncontrollably into his hands. Rose knelt before him, gently lifting his head, her hands cradling his face. "Dave, I'm here," she whispered. "You haven't failed me. You'll never lose me." Her words were a lifeline thrown into the stormy sea of his emotions.

No more words were needed. They embraced, a silent understanding passing between them, tears mingling, hearts beating as one.

In that moment, time seemed to stand still. Dave felt a flicker of hope ignite within him, a tiny spark amidst the darkness that threatened to consume him. Rose's unwavering love and support were like a beacon, guiding him back from the brink.

As they held each other, Dave felt the weight of his burdens begin to lift, if only slightly. He knew that the road ahead would be difficult, that healing would take time, but with Rose by his side, he felt that he could face whatever challenges lay ahead.

Eventually, they pulled away from each other, their eyes meeting in a silent exchange of love and determination. Rose helped Dave to his feet, her touch gentle yet firm. "We'll get through this together," she said, her voice filled with conviction.

Dave nodded, a faint smile tugging at the corners of his lips. For the first time in what felt like forever, he felt a glimmer of hope. With Rose by his side, he knew that he could overcome anything.

Over the next several weeks, Dave and Rose's love story unfolded like a beautifully scripted novel. Every moment they spent together seemed to deepen their bond, strengthening the foundation of their relationship. As they worked side by side to rebuild their home, they also began to envision the perfect wedding day, a day that would symbolize their love and commitment to each other.

Their wedding planning became a labor of love, a shared project that brought them even closer together. They poured over every detail, from the flavor of the wedding cake to the intricate design of the invitations. Together, they decided on a vanilla salted caramel wedding cake that would serve over 400 guests, a choice that perfectly captured their sweet and enduring love.

To ensure that their dream wedding became a reality, Dave and Rose spared no expense. They hired the world's best wedding decorators, each one bringing a unique touch to the event. The decorations were exquisite, creating a magical atmosphere that would be remembered for years to come.

As they finalized the seating arrangements and put the finishing touches on their plans, Dave and Rose couldn't help but feel a sense of awe. This wedding was more than just a celebration of their love; it was a testament to their strength and resilience.

Together, they had overcome so much, and now they were about to embark on a new chapter of their lives, hand in hand, united in love and commitment.

The date had been circled on the calendar, and now, with RSVPs flooding in from all corners of the globe, the excitement in Dave and Rose's eyes was tremendous. Family, friends, and clients, all eager to witness their union, responded one after the other, confirming their attendance. Dave and Rose could barely contain their anticipation for the big day.

With everything meticulously arranged, Dave and Rose decided to spend the evening indulging in what they loved most about their island home. They packed a picnic and headed to their favorite beach, a secluded spot where they had shared countless intimate moments. As the sun dipped below the horizon, painting the sky in shades of pink and orange, they sat side by side, savoring the beauty of the moment.

But for Dave, this beach held a deeper significance, one that he had kept buried deep within him. It was here, on this very beach, that he had reached his lowest point. The night when the grip of alcohol had clouded his judgment, pushing him to the edge of despair. It was the same night he had walked into the ocean, consumed by thoughts of never resurfacing.

As Rose glanced over at Dave, she noticed his distant gaze fixed on the rolling waves. Concerned, she asked, "What is it, Dave?" He didn't respond at first, lost in the memories that still haunted him. "Dave?" Rose's voice was tinged with worry. Finally, he turned to her, his eyes filled with a mixture of guilt and relief. "I thought I lost you," he began, his voice barely above a whisper. "I know you said I didn't, but deep down, I thought I did."

Tears welled up in Rose's eyes as she listened to him bare his soul. She reached out and took his hand, a silent gesture of support. "I hate ruining moments, moments with you," Dave continued, his voice trembling. "But while you were in Spain with your mother, alcohol consumed my mind. It controlled me." Rose's heart ached at the pain he had endured in silence.

"I walked into the ocean as far as I could and let the waves take me," Dave confessed, his voice breaking. "I wanted peace, comfort, and the pain to go away. But I came to the realization that you are my savior, my hope, my will to live." Rose was speechless, her mind reeling from the revelation. "You tried to commit suicide?" she asked, her voice barely audible.

Dave nodded, his eyes filled with remorse. "Yes," he replied softly. He went on to explain that it wasn't him, but the alcohol that had driven him to such drastic measures. In that moment, he made a promise to himself, a promise that he swore to keep for the rest of his life - the promise of never drinking again.

For the rest of the evening, Dave and Rose lay on the beach in each other's arms, silent but content. The sun dipped below the horizon, casting a warm glow over the sea. The gentle sound of the waves provided a soothing backdrop to their thoughts. They never revisited the topic of Dave's attempted suicide, silently agreeing to leave those dark moments behind and focus on building a stronger future together.

Several months flew by, filled with excitement and anticipation for the upcoming wedding. Rose traveled back to Spain to pick up her royal princess dress, a breathtaking creation that would be the centerpiece of their special day. Carefully packing it for the journey back to the island, she couldn't help but smile at the thought of walking down the aisle to Dave.

Once reunited, Dave and Rose threw themselves into the final preparations with fervor. They worked closely with the wedding designers, ensuring every detail was perfect. From the flowers to the seating arrangements, they wanted everything to be just right for their guests.

As the wedding day approached, guests began to arrive on the island, greeted with warm smiles and open arms. The villas that Dave and Rose had remodeled and prepared for their stay were a luxurious home away from home. Each guest was treated like royalty, ensuring they felt welcome and appreciated.

Finally, the day arrived. Dave and Rose woke up to a beautiful sunrise, nerves and excitement bubbling within them. As they got ready, surrounded by their closest friends and family, they couldn't help but feel grateful for the journey that had brought them to this moment.

There was one last surprise that Rose prepared for Dave. She was nervous to see his reaction, unsure if he might be mad at her decision. As Dave stood on the outer edge, waiting for Rose to walk down the aisle to him, he noticed two people in the seating. "MOM? DAD?" Dave yelled softly. Rose had tracked down his adoptive parents, whom he had lost contact with years ago, and invited them to the wedding. At first, Dave was confused. "How are they here?" he thought to himself. But then a feeling of joy overtook him. Since Dave had no blood relatives who ever wanted him after the death of his father and later his mother, his adoptive parents were the only close family he had.

Then the wedding began. First, all the wedding party came down the aisle with Rose's nieces as flower girls, paving the way for Rose in abundance amounts of rose petals. Then Rose came down the aisle, led by her mother. Dave was blown away by Rose's beauty; he could barely keep himself controlled. His heart overflowing with love and gratitude, couldn't wait to express his feelings to Rose. As they stood facing each other, surrounded by their loved ones, he began:

"Rose, from the moment I met you, I knew you were special. You've brought so much light and love into my life, and I can't imagine a day without you by my side. I promise to cherish and support you, to laugh with you in good times and to hold you in the bad. I vow to be your partner in all things, to listen and to learn, to be there for you in every way possible. I love you more than words can say, and I can't wait to spend forever with you."

Rose, her eyes brimming with tears of happiness, took Dave's hands in hers and said:

"Dave, you are my rock, my soulmate, my everything. From the moment I met you, I knew my life would never be the same. You've shown me what true love is, and I am so grateful to have you in my life. I promise to stand by your side through thick and thin, to support and encourage you in all your dreams. I vow to be your partner in every sense of the word, to love and cherish you for all eternity. I love you more than anything in this world, and I can't wait to start this new chapter of our lives together."

With those words, they exchanged rings, sealing their love and commitment to each other. As they kissed, surrounded by their friends and family, they knew that this was only the beginning of their beautiful journey together. The reception was filled with laughter, tears, and dancing. Dave's parents reconnected with him, and they shared stories and memories that filled the room with warmth.

# Chapter Seven

A few days after their wedding, as the final guests waved goodbye, Dave and Rose began packing for their honeymoon in Bora Bora. They were filled with excitement about the adventure ahead. The journey was long and involved multiple flights and layovers, but the anticipation kept their spirits high.

On their first day, they took time to rest and recover from the journey. That evening, they had a romantic dinner and walked the beach, relishing each other's company as newlyweds. Dave and Rose couldn't believe they were finally married. They had already faced so much together in such a short time, more than some experience in a lifetime. But these challenges had only strengthened their bond, making them better partners for life.

Later that night, lying in bed, Dave turned to Rose, holding her hand. "Rose, I think we should start a family," he said softly. Rose's heart constricted at the memory of her heartbreaking miscarriage. "Dave, I was shattered after we lost our baby," she replied, her voice heavy with emotion. "We didn't even know I was pregnant, and it destroyed me. I don't think I could survive another loss after knowing I'm pregnant."

Dave promised Rose, the world's best doctor, that they wouldn't try for a baby until they were certain they wouldn't have to worry. The weight of their decision lingered between them, casting a subtle shadow over the rest of the evening. They exchanged few words, each lost in their own thoughts, the silence punctuated only by the gentle lapping of waves against the shore.

The next morning, Dave woke Rose with a luxurious breakfast in bed to start her day with love and happiness. "Good morning, my beautiful wife," Dave said to Rose, his smile radiating happiness as he planted a soft kiss on her forehead. Rose felt a wave of love wash over her; she was in heaven.

After Dave had prepared and handed her breakfast, he announced, "I'll be back soon," with excitement evident in his voice. "Aren't you eating with me?" Rose inquired. Dave replied, "This is yours, baby, but I'll be back before you finish." Rose was puzzled but noticed Dave's excitement and kissed him goodbye.

About twenty minutes later, Dave returned. By then, Rose had finished eating and was up and ready for the day. Dave took Rose's hand and asked her to come with him. "Where are we going?" she asked. "Follow me, and you'll soon see," he replied, his eyes twinkling with joy.

Dave led Rose down to the water's edge, where a small boat awaited them. "We're going snorkeling," Dave announced, his face beaming with excitement. Rose's eyes widened with delight. She had always wanted to try snorkeling, and here, in the crystal-clear waters of Bora Bora, it was the perfect opportunity.

As they sailed out to sea, Rose marveled at the beauty of the island. The water was a stunning shade of turquoise, and the sun shone brightly overhead. Dave looked at Rose, his heart full of love. When they arrived at the snorkeling spot, Dave helped Rose into the water. She was amazed at the vibrant coral reefs and the colorful fish that swam around her. Dave swam by her side, pointing out different species and marveling at the beauty of the underwater world. After an hour of snorkeling, Dave led Rose back to the boat, where a picnic lunch awaited them. They sat on the deck, eating and laughing, enjoying each other's company.

Later that evening, the sultry island air wrapped around

them as they stepped into the night, heading towards a local restaurant alive with the vibrant sounds of live music. The melody, a lively rhythm of guitars and drums, seemed to pull at Dave's heartstrings, infusing him with a sense of joy and freedom.

As they settled at their table, the music surrounded them, setting a lively backdrop for their meal. Dave couldn't resist the urge to dance with Rose, his heart full and his spirits high. Standing up, he extended his hand towards her, a silent invitation that spoke volumes of his love and desire. "Dance with me?" he asked, a playful smile dancing on his lips as he gently pulled her up from her seat. Rose's eyes sparkled with delight as she accepted his hand, letting him lead her to the center of the room. The dance floor seemed to come alive beneath their feet, the music guiding their movements as they swayed in perfect harmony. Their laughter mingled with the sweet melody, creating a moment that felt like it could last forever.

After the enchanting dance, they strolled back to their room, the night alive with the sounds of the island. Dave had orchestrated a scene of pure romance, the room filled with the soft glow of candles and the sweet scent of flowers. Rose's heart swelled at the sight, her love for Dave overflowing.

Turning towards him, her eyes shining with love, she whispered, "Make love to me," her voice barely audible over the soft crackle of the flames.

Dave's heart skipped a beat at her words, his desire for her burning brighter than ever. With a tender smile, he pulled her into his arms, his touch gentle yet firm as he kissed her passionately, his hands exploring every curve of her body. They moved together, their bodies entwined in a dance as old as time, their love for each other igniting a fire that burned hotter with each passing moment.

In that intimate embrace, they lost themselves in each other, their love transcending the physical as they became one, their souls merging in a moment of pure bliss. And as they lay tangled in each other's arms, spent and satisfied, they knew that this night would be etched in their hearts forever, a memory of a love that knew no bounds.

Over the next several days, Dave and Rose's honeymoon in Bora Bora unfolded like a dream. Each morning, they woke up in their luxurious overwater bungalow, the gentle lapping of the waves against the stilts lulling them into a peaceful awakening.

Eager to explore, they set out to hike the island, guided by a local expert who regaled them with stories of the island's history and secrets. Together, they traversed rugged terrain and dense forests, discovering hidden waterfalls and ancient ruins along the way. Dave and Rose were in awe of the natural beauty surrounding them, feeling as though they had stepped into a paradise untouched by time.

During their hikes, they encountered local wildlife, from colorful birds to playful monkeys, adding to the magic of their experience. They paused often to take in the breathtaking views, the vast expanse of the ocean stretching out before them, a vivid blue canvas against the clear sky.

When they weren't hiking, Dave and Rose spent their days indulging in the island's delights. They dined on exquisite cuisine, sampling a variety of dishes made from fresh, local ingredients. Each meal was a culinary adventure, with flavors and aromas that tantalized their taste buds and left them craving more.

In the evenings, they danced under the stars, the soft glow of torches lighting their way. The rhythm of the music filled them with joy, and they moved together as though they had been dancing together for a lifetime.

They also embarked on thrilling boat adventures, exploring the island's hidden coves and pristine beaches. They went parasailing, soaring high above the island, the wind in their hair and the sun on their faces. They laughed and shouted, feeling free and alive in each other's company.

Dave had planned every detail of their honeymoon, wanting only the best for Rose. He wanted this time together to be a celebration of their love, a chance for them to create memories that would last a lifetime.

As the final days of their honeymoon approached, Dave and Rose found themselves caught in a bittersweet whirlwind of memories. They spent long hours reminiscing about the adventures they had shared, the quiet moments of connection, and the deep, abiding love that had blossomed between them.

Each day seemed to pass too quickly, filled with laughter, exploration, and a profound sense of togetherness. They discovered new facets of each other's personalities, deepening their bond with every passing moment. As they looked back on these precious days, they knew without a doubt that they were meant to be together.

Their conversations often turned to the future, to the life they would build together. They talked about their dreams and aspirations and the adventures they would embark on. They knew that whatever challenges life threw their way, they would face them together, with love, loyalty, and unwavering support.

As they spent their final days relaxing on the beach, the world around them seemed to fade away, leaving only the two of them in their own paradise. They drew hearts in the sand, with their names in the middle, a symbol of the love that bound them together.

When the time came to leave, they gathered their belongings and headed to the airport, their hearts heavy with the knowledge that their honeymoon was coming to an end. But as they waited at the gate, hand in hand, they knew that this was just the beginning of their journey together. And as they boarded the plane, ready to embark on the next chapter of their lives, they were filled with excitement for the future and the adventures that lay ahead.

A few moments after the cabin door shut, the captain's voice crackled over the intercom, announcing with a hint of apology that due to a faulty sensor, they would need to wait for maintenance to come and repair the plane before they could take off. The passengers groaned collectively, shifting in their seats as they resigned themselves to the delay. The crew assured everyone that it should be a quick fix, and they would be on their way shortly.

However, as minutes turned into hours, the mood inside the plane grew increasingly restless. The initial hum of conversation died down, replaced by sighs and the occasional frustrated murmur. Flight attendants walked up and down the aisle, offering snacks and drinks to keep spirits up, but it did little to alleviate the growing impatience.

Dave and Rose, seated near the front of the plane, tried to make the best of the situation. Dave cracked jokes to keep Rose entertained, but even his humor couldn't mask their growing frustration. Then Rose had an idea. She suggested they call home and leave a loving message on their answering machine. Dialing the number, she waited for the machine to pick up. When it was time to speak, she held the phone between Dave and herself and began, "Hey guys, this is us from the past! On our way home." She giggled slightly, nudging Dave, "Dave, say something."

Dave gazed into her eyes and said, "Hey future me, you're now married to the most beautiful person in the world. Treat her with love, respect, and make her your priority for life. See you soon." Rose ended the call with laughter and love, feeling the warmth of their bond consume them.

Finally, after what felt like an eternity, the captain's voice came over the intercom again, this time with a tone of relief. Maintenance had fixed the issue, and they were cleared for departure. A collective cheer went up from the passengers, and

Dave squeezed Rose's hand, a smile spreading across his face. They were finally on their way home.

They took off, the plane ascending into the sky as they began their journey home. The cabin was filled with a mix of relief and nostalgia; their honeymoon in Bora Bora had been a dream. Dave glanced at Rose, her smile radiant as she gazed out the window at the receding island below.

As the plane leveled off, the flight attendants began their routine, offering drinks and snacks to the passengers. Dave leaned back in his seat, content and relaxed while holding Rose's hand.

Before takeoff, the captain's voice came over the intercom, announcing their route would take them through a storm. Despite this, he reassured the passengers that the crew would do their utmost to ensure a smooth and relaxing flight. However, as the plane ascended into the turbulent skies, it became clear that the storm was more formidable than anticipated.

# Chapter Eight

"ROSE! ROSE, WHERE ARE YOU?"

The deafening roar of the crashing waves was matched only by the chaos inside the plane. Metal groaned and shattered as the aircraft tore apart upon impact with the ocean. Dave struggled against the force of the impact, desperate to find Rose amidst the wreckage.

His promise echoed in his mind: he wouldn't let go. But the violent jolt had ripped her from his grasp. As he called out her name, fear clenched his heart. The memory of their tender moments in Bora Bora flooded his thoughts, a cruel contrast to the nightmare unfolding around him

Through the haze of shock and confusion, Dave searched frantically. Smoke billowed, obscuring his vision, but he pushed forward, driven by love and desperation. Rose had to be here somewhere, she just had to be, but Dave never found her.

Dave felt a crushing weight of emotion, heavier than any he had ever experienced. It was worse than the day his father died in a drunk driving accident, worse than the day the state took him from his mother as a child, and even worse than the day his mother took her own life. Each memory flooded his mind, each loss stacking upon the other until it felt like the weight of the world was on his shoulders.

Rose had been his beacon of hope, the one person who had shown him genuine love and care. Her smile was the sun breaking through the clouds on a rainy day, her touch a comforting embrace that chased away his darkest fears. She had saved him in more ways than one, pulling him from the depths of despair and showing him that life was worth living.

As he laid in the wreckage, battered and broken, Dave was on the brink of giving up. The pain of his injuries paled in comparison to the ache in his heart, the overwhelming sense of loss threatening to consume him. But a flicker of hope remained, a desperate belief that maybe, just maybe, Rose was still alive. He clung to that fragile thread, unwilling to let go, even as tears streamed down his face, mixing with the rain.

He called out her name, his voice hoarse and desperate, hoping that she would answer. But there was only silence, broken only by the sound of his own ragged breathing. And in that moment, Dave felt more alone than he ever had before, the magnitude of his loss crashing down on him like a tidal wave.

But somewhere, deep down, a small voice whispered that it wasn't over yet. That as long as he had breath in his body, there was still a chance. And so, with every ounce of strength he could muster, Dave pushed aside his pain and his grief, and vowed to keep fighting, if not for himself, then for the woman he loved more than life itself.

Dave clung desperately to the life jacket he had found bobbing in the water, the only thing keeping him afloat amidst the vast expanse of the ocean. Every breath was a struggle, the salty air burning his lungs.

"Rose!" he cried out once more hoping to catch a glimpse of her, but there was nothing. The ocean stretched out endlessly, devoid of any signs of life.

Hours passed, marked only by the slow descent of the sun towards the horizon. The flames that had engulfed the plane were long gone, leaving behind a trail of debris scattered across the sea. Dave's strength was waning, the combination of exhaustion, dehydration, and despair taking its toll.

Still, he refused to give up hope. He called out for Rose again and again, his voice growing weaker with each attempt. As the darkness of night began to fall, Dave felt himself being carried away by the gentle currents, his body too tired to resist. .

As Dave swam through the debris and bodies of passengers, he realized the gravity of the situation. Hours passed as he searched, feeling broken and defeated. Eventually, overcome by exhaustion and his injuries, Dave had no choice but to give up his search. As he felt the cold water rushing over him, he resigned himself to what he believed was the end.

But just when all seemed lost, he felt a hand pulling him up from beneath the waves, though no one was visible. Then, a bright light pierced the darkness, a search and rescue helicopter appeared overhead, its powerful beam cutting through the night. Dave's heart leaped with hope as he was pulled from the water and onto the safety of the helicopter.

As he was flown to safety, Dave clung to the slim chance that Rose had also been rescued, that she was waiting for him on the shore. But as the days passed and there was no sign of her, the truth began to sink in. Rose was gone, lost to the depths of the ocean.

Heartbroken, Dave returned home, haunted by the memories of his lost love. But amidst the pain, he found a glimmer of peace, knowing that Rose would always be with him, guiding him through the darkest of times. And as he looked out at the vast expanse of the ocean, he whispered her name, a tribute to the love they had shared and the love that would never die.

Dave traveled to Spain, a country filled with memories of Rose. Every corner seemed to whisper her name, and every street held a piece of their shared history. He arrived at the airport, a place once filled with joy and anticipation, now a stark reminder of his loss.

As he waited, time seemed to stand still. The bustle of the airport faded into the background, leaving Dave alone with his thoughts. His emotions were a tumultuous mix of sorrow and longing, the weight of his grief almost too much to bear.

When he finally mustered the strength to approach Rose's family, his heart felt heavy. He knew that seeing them would bring both comfort and pain. Dave's face was a mask of sadness, his eyes betraying the deep sorrow he felt inside. He was silent, words failing to convey the depth of his emotions.

The journey to Rose's mother's home was a blur. Dave walked, his body moving on instinct alone. His mind was consumed with memories of Rose, each step bringing him closer to the past they had shared.

Arriving at the house, Dave hesitated before knocking. The reality of the moment hit him hard, and he took a moment to collect himself. When Rose's sister, Sofia, answered the door, Dave was overwhelmed with emotion. Without a word, Sofia pulled him into a tight embrace, and Dave felt a flood of memories wash over him.

Tears streamed down his face as Sofia spoke softly, her words a balm to his wounded heart. "Dave, she loved you so much," Sofia whispered. "You meant the world to her." Her words pierced his soul, and Dave felt a deep sense of loss wash over him.

He sank to the ground, his body racked with sobs, as Sofia continued to hold him. In that moment, Dave realized that he was not alone in his grief. He was surrounded by people who loved Rose, people who shared his pain and his memories.

Sofia gently guided Dave into the home, her touch a grounding force amidst the sea of grief that consumed them. The once vibrant house, where Dave had shared countless happy moments with Rose, now felt unfamiliar and hollow. The air was heavy with unspoken sorrow, the sounds of laughter and music replaced by stifled sobs and hushed conversations.

As they walked through the house, Dave was greeted by somber faces and embraces filled with both sympathy and shared loss. Each hug and condolence offered only served to deepen his sense of loss.

Despite the heartfelt condolences, there was a noticeable absence. Rose's mother, the matriarch of the family, was nowhere to be seen. Dave's heart ached at the thought of her grief, knowing how deeply she must be suffering. He longed to offer her some comfort, to share in her pain as he had with the rest of the family, but she remained elusive.

After spending some time with the family, sharing stories and memories of Rose, Dave felt a familiar sense of restlessness creeping in. He knew he had to leave before his emotions overwhelmed him. As he made his way towards the front door, a soft sound caught his attention.

At the end of the hallway, a door stood slightly open, and through the crack, Dave could hear gentle cries. He approached the door and peeked inside. There, sitting alone in the dimly lit room, was Rose's mother.

The sight of her sitting there, lost in her grief, brought back memories of his own mother's sorrow after his father's death. He remembered the pain in her eyes, the emptiness that seemed to consume her. Dave felt a surge of empathy for Rose's mother, knowing all too well the depth of her sorrow.

As he turned to leave, Rose's mother's voice called out to him, breaking the silence. "Dave?" she said. "Please come in."

Dave hesitated for a moment before stepping into the room. He took a seat beside her, and without a word, he reached out and took her hand in his. They sat there in silence, two souls united in grief.

In that moment, Dave realized that grief was not something to be endured alone. It was a burden that could be shared, a pain that could be eased by the simple act of being there for one another. And as he sat there with Rose's mother, he knew that in their shared sorrow, they had found a connection that would help them both heal.

Dave stayed a while longer, finding comfort in the presence of family as they discussed the funeral arrangements. The decision to hold the service on the island felt right, a fitting tribute to Rose, whose spirit seemed to linger in every corner of their paradise.

The funeral was an intimate affair, attended only by immediate family and their closest friends. It was a somber gathering, made more poignant by the fact that just a few weeks earlier, the same group had joyously celebrated Dave and Rose's wedding on these very shores.

After the service, the group made their way to the beach, a place that held so many memories of Dave and Rose's love story. Without Rose's ashes to scatter—cremation being uncommon in Spain and impossible without her body—they decided on a different kind of tribute. Each family member took a handful of rose petals, symbolizing Rose's name and essence, and one by one, they cast them into the gentle waves, accompanied by quiet prayers and words of love. Dave led the ceremony, his heart heavy with grief yet filled with a deep sense of gratitude for having known and loved Rose.

As the sun began to set Dave stood by the water's edge, watching as the petals floated away, carried by the tide. In that moment, surrounded by love and memories, he felt a sense of peace, knowing that Rose's spirit would always be with him, forever a part of the island they had both cherished so dearly.

After the funeral, the bustle of departing friends gradually faded, leaving Dave on the island with Rose's family. They lingered, offering support and ensuring Dave was coping with his loss. His days fell into a rhythm of solitude, spent gazing out at the ocean, aching for Rose's return, a presence he knew was forever lost to him.

The nights were the hardest. Sleep became a stranger, replaced by haunting nightmares of the accident and the void it left in his life. Rose's mother tried to ease his pain, but some wounds run too deep for mere words.

As days turned into weeks, even family began to depart, leaving Dave to face the island's emptiness alone. The once-beloved surroundings now felt alien, devoid of the life and love that once filled them. His home, once a sanctuary, now echoed with the silence of his grief, a stark reminder of all he had lost.

One afternoon, as Dave sat on the beach, the bottle of bourbon caught his eye. It was a remnant of happier times, a symbol of celebrations and shared moments with Rose. The temptation to drown his sorrows in its contents was strong, but he hesitated, remembering the promise he had made to himself and to Rose never to touch alcohol again.

"What's the point now?" a voice whispered in his mind, but he quickly silenced it. He couldn't betray Rose's memory, not after all they had shared. With a heavy sigh, he placed the bottle back down, determined to honor her memory by staying true to himself, even in the face of unbearable loss.

Dave sat, tears blurring the island's beauty. Hours passed, each minute heavier with the weight of loss. He was adrift, clinging to memories that danced like ghosts, each one a piece of Rose.

In these memories, smiles flickered, moments of joy that now seemed distant and fragile. But they were overshadowed by the stark reality of her absence. Dave knew he needed to move forward, to find a path through the grief that consumed him, but the way was shrouded in darkness.

The island, once a haven, now felt like a prison of memories. He couldn't bear to part with it, a place where Rose's spirit lingered in every corner. Their home was a testament to their love, a place where they had weathered storms and celebrated triumphs. Selling it felt like betraying her memory, erasing the life they had built together.

Dave was lost, unsure of how to begin the journey back to himself. The island held him in its hands, a reminder of all he had lost and all he had loved. He needed to find a way to honor Rose's memory while also finding a way to move forward.

As the sun began to set, casting a golden glow over the island, Dave made a decision. He would stay, not out of fear or obligation, but out of love. He would stay to honor Rose's memory, to keep alive the love they had shared. And maybe, just maybe, in the quiet moments between the waves and the wind, he would find a way to begin again.

# Chapter Nine

Several weeks after Rose's death, Dave reluctantly returned to work, his heart heavy with grief. His employees noticed the change in him and tried their best to restore a sense of normalcy, but Dave's world had been shattered.

Dave's job required him to travel, visiting his stores around the world. It was a routine he had once enjoyed, but now each trip felt like a painful reminder of his loss. The thought of attending auctions was especially unbearable.

Rose had been the life of the auctions, her smile lighting up the room as she bid on items with enthusiasm. Dave couldn't imagine going to an auction without her by his side, her presence now a painful absence.

Instead, Dave threw himself into his work, using it as a distraction from his grief. He traveled from store to store, avoiding the island that had once been theirs, now a lonely reminder of what he had lost. The island held too many memories, too many echoes of their happiness together.

Dave longed for the day when he could return home and not feel the overwhelming emptiness that now consumed him. But for now, he continued to travel, each day a struggle to find a sense of purpose without Rose by his side.

Dave's home store was in Spain, a picturesque location he had chosen to be closer to Rose after they fell in love. The quaint store nestled in a charming alleyway held memories of their early days together, making it a place he couldn't bring himself to visit since her passing. Despite being in Spain since her death, he couldn't shake the feeling of sadness and longing that engulfed him whenever he thought about that store.

Although his other stores were thriving and managed well in his absence, Dave found himself traveling between them for several months, unable to return home to their island. He would spend nights at the stores, immersing himself in work to keep his mind occupied and avoid confronting the pain of losing Rose.

One evening in Paris, Dave found himself on a familiar bench in front of the Eiffel Tower, a spot he frequented before meeting Rose and one they cherished together. However, on this particular evening, the usually vibrant lights of the tower remained off, casting a somber mood over the area as misty rain fell around him. Sitting there, staring at the dark silhouette of the tower against the night sky, Dave was struck by a profound realization.

In that moment, he decided that he would sell all of his stores around the world. He no longer felt the need to hold on to them, especially with the memories of Rose attached. He needed a fresh start, a clean slate that didn't remind him of his past life with her. He knew that he couldn't hide from the island forever, and the constant travel between stores was no longer healthy. It was time to let go and move forward, even if it meant saying goodbye to the businesses he had worked so hard to build.

Dave started on a gradual process of selling his stores, some worth millions, at steep discounts. Money was no issue; he just wanted a fresh start, a new chapter that would bring peace of mind.

All but one store, in Spain, remained. Dave decided to gift it to Rose's family. They didn't need the money, but he believed they would care for it well. He signed over the store and all its inventory to them.

On the eve of the transfer, Dave built the strength to visit the store. Memories flooded back as he wandered, recalling the joyous times with Rose. In the vault, he stumbled upon a surprise. "The Birkin Bag?" he exclaimed, the symbol of his first encounter with Rose, the beginning of their journey together.

The bag held too much sentimental value to sell. It was a reminder of the love he shared with Rose. Dave decided to leave it, showcasing it in the store as a tribute, not for sale. Holding the bag, conflicting emotions washed over him. "I should never have bought this bag," he lamented, believing that its purchase had led to Rose's death.

But then a wave of selfishness engulfed him. The thought of never meeting Rose saddened him deeply. The bag was a vessel of myriad emotions, leaving him unsure of what to do next.

As he stood in the store, memories flooded back. The Birkin Bag was more than just a bag; it was a symbol of their love, their hopes, and their dreams.

Dave realized that selling the bag would be like selling a part of himself, a part of the life he had shared with Rose. He decided to keep the bag, not as a reminder of what he had lost, but as a reminder of what he had gained - a love that would last a lifetime, no matter what.

Dave carefully packed the bag, his movements deliberate and measured, each fold and tuck a silent vow to the future he was determined to forge. As he zipped it shut, a sudden resolve settled within him like a cloak. It was time to return to the island, to the place where every breeze whispered Rose's name and every wave carried her memory. The future loomed uncertain, but he was firm in his commitment to survive and honor her legacy. He knew he had to focus on himself, to keep moving forward not just for himself, but for Rose, for the life they had planned together. The thought of her presence, a guiding light in the darkness of his grief, gave him strength.

He arranged for his private jet to be fueled and ready for his arrival, a mode of travel he hadn't used in a long time. Rose had always loved the thrill of commercial flights, the sense of adventure they brought, but today, he needed the solitude and familiarity of his own aircraft. With the bag securely by his side, he bid a tearful farewell to Rose's family and headed towards the airport.

At the airport, his pilots greeted him warmly, their expressions a mix of sympathy and respect, happy to have him back on board. His favorite meal was prepared and waiting for him by the stewardess, a simple yet poignant gesture that touched him deeply. Dave settled into his favorite seat, the plush leather cradling him like an old friend, as he savored his meal and prepared himself for the journey ahead.

Just before the plane lifted off, the pilot approached him, kneeling down beside his seat and placing a hand on Dave's shoulder. "I'm sorry for your loss, Dave. We all loved her and truly miss her," the pilot said softly, his eyes reflecting the sadness they all felt.

Dave swallowed hard, the lump in his throat threatening to overwhelm him, and thanked the pilot for his kind words. As the jet soared into the sky, leaving the city lights far below, Dave gazed out the window, the memories of Rose overcoming his mind like a bittersweet symphony. But amid the pain and the longing, he felt her presence, a gentle presence that was full of love and hope, guiding him forward into the vast unknown that lay ahead.

Several hours later, Dave arrived back home to his island, the weight of the day heavy on his shoulders. Opening the front door slowly, he stepped inside, greeted by the familiar sights and sounds of home. He hung up his jacket and placed his wallet and keys on the decorative table in the hallway, a piece Rose had chosen just days before their honeymoon. As he walked away, he ran his hand over the table, seeking a trace of Rose's presence, a comfort that now felt fleeting.

The house was quiet, the lights dimmed, and a chill hung in the air. Dave wandered into the kitchen and poured himself a glass of ice water, the coolness soothing against his parched throat. The answering machine blinked with a full inbox, filled with messages offering condolences for Rose's loss. Dave knew these calls were well-intentioned, but he couldn't bear to listen to them. Before he deleted them all, he remembered the message he and Rose had left while waiting for the flight that would forever change his world and lead to the loss of Rose.

After listening to all the messages, he finally reached the one he needed to hear. He wanted to hear Rose's beautiful, loving voice once more. However, when he played the message, it wasn't what he expected. There were only a few words. "Can you hear me?" It was Rose's voice, but there were no further messages.

Dave realized that when they had called, the message hadn't recorded properly, and Rose must have accidentally dialed again, unaware that the first message hadn't been captured. Despite feeling sadness that the message he had hoped for was not there, he was grateful for the few words he had in Rose's voice, a precious reminder of her.

Feeling a mix of emotions, Dave went to the balcony and watched as night descended, the stars twinkling above. Eventually, he retreated to the living room, where he laid on the couch, staring at the ceiling, lost in thoughts of Rose. Slowly, he drifted off to sleep, the memories of his beloved wife filling his dreams.

The next morning Dave woke to the gentle melody of Rose's favorite song, the soft notes floating through the air and coaxing him out of his slumber. Blinking away sleep, he sat up on the couch, his heart stirring with a mix of confusion.

Following the music's trail, Dave made his way to the bedroom, the melody growing louder and more distinct with each step. "Hello?" he called out, his voice wavering slightly as he pushed open the bedroom door. The room was bathed in soft morning light, the curtains fluttering in the breeze, but there was no one there.

His gaze fell upon the record player, the vinyl spinning slowly, playing the familiar tune. Dave approached the player, his movements slow and deliberate, as if afraid to disturb the moment. He lifted the arm of the player, the music abruptly stopping, leaving behind an eerie silence.

Standing there, holding the record sleeve in his hand, Dave felt a chill run down his spine. Was this a sign? A message from Rose? Lost in thought, he was jolted back to reality by the ringing of his phone. Startled, he replaced the record, leaving the room to answer the call.

On the other end was Rose's mother, her voice filled with concern and warmth. She wanted to check on Dave, to make sure he had returned home safely. Dave assured her that he was fine, but as he hung up the phone, he couldn't shake the feeling that Rose was trying to tell him something, reaching out to him from beyond the grave.

Dave spent the day exploring the island, his footsteps leaving imprints on the sandy paths as he checked on all the villas and the resort. His absence had coincided with a few storms, but as he looked around, there was no sign of any significant damage. Satisfied, he returned to his home and settled in for the evening.

As the sun dipped below the horizon, casting a warm glow over the island, Dave found himself drawn to the deck overlooking the ocean. The gentle sound of waves lapping against the shore was a soothing backdrop to his thoughts. He couldn't shake the memory of the mysterious incident earlier that morning—the haunting melody of Rose's favorite song playing on the recorder, seemingly by itself.

Despite the peaceful surroundings, a sense of unease lingered. Dave tried to distract himself, flipping through channels on the TV and browsing through books, but his mind kept returning to the inexplicable event. Was it just a coincidence, or was there something more to it?

As the night wore on, the quiet of the island surrounded him, amplifying every creak and rustle. Dave couldn't shake the feeling of being watched, of unseen eyes following his every move. He tried to dismiss it as paranoia, but the memory of the music playing in the empty room haunted him.

Eventually, exhaustion took over, and Dave retired to bed, hoping that sleep would bring clarity to his troubled mind

# Chapter Ten

A few weeks had passed, and Dave started to feel more normal after losing Rose. Yet, the hurt lingered in his heart. There was still a piece missing. Each day had become a bit easier to get through, but he pushed on, knowing that's what Rose would have wanted.

One early morning, Dave decided it was time to go through Rose's belongings. Although he wasn't ready to remove any of her things, he thought he could begin boxing and organizing them. He started with her jewelry. Jewelry was a big part of Dave's life, as it was what created his fortune. The jewelry industry is also what brought him to Rose.

As he started emptying the drawers of her jewelry box, he noticed something very familiar. "It can't be," he spoke out loud. There it was, Rose's wedding band. This struck Dave by surprise because he was certain it was on her finger at the time of the plane wreck. "It was on her finger when she was lost at sea," he thought to himself.

Taking a few steps back with the ring in his hand, he just stared at it, his face expressionless. "How can this be?" Dave thought. At this point, Dave snapped, second-guessing his reality. He put the ring in his pocket and ran through every room of the house, yelling her name, "Rose," frantically searching.

Dave ran out of the house, all through the island, down to the beach, yelling for Rose, but she was nowhere to be found. In his mind, this didn't make any sense. Rose would have never come back if she was alive without finding Dave.

Dave made it all the way to the beach where he collapsed, screaming and crying so loudly that all the birds flew from the trees. He laid there with his head in the sand, crying, as none of this made sense.

After a while, he sat himself up with his back against a rock and put his hand in his pocket to retrieve the ring. But it was gone. Frantically, he searched his pocket, pulling it inside out, but it was gone. Quickly, he returned to his feet, looking all around in the sand, but did not find it.

Dave ran back to the house, retracing his steps, never leaving his eyes off the ground, but yet the ring was still missing. Dave was at a loss. The ring was clearly in his hands; there was no way he could have imagined it. But after he searched everywhere, including the jewelry box, he second-guessed himself. It must have been a mirage of his own mind.

Dave felt lost, his thoughts a tangled mess. He needed help, someone who understood Rose like no one else—her mother. With a sense of urgency, Dave summoned his pilots and readied himself for a flight to Spain. Time was slipping away, and he couldn't afford to delay.

The pilots swiftly prepared the plane, and Dave arrived at the airport, his mind consumed by memories of Rose. Once in the air, he remained silent, his gaze fixed on the passing landscape. His thoughts replayed moments with Rose: the eerie play of her favorite record, the mysterious disappearance of her wedding band. These inexplicable occurrences haunted him, defying any rational explanation.

Once Dave arrived in Spain, his drivers were waiting for

him. Anxious and restless, he quickly got into the car and directed them to Rose's mother's home. The drive was a blur, the passing scenery unnoticed as Dave's mind raced with thoughts of Rose. It felt like an eternity, but finally, they arrived. Dave practically leaped out of the vehicle and hurried to the door, his heart pounding with a mix of anxiety and anticipation. He knocked eagerly, the sound echoing in the quiet street, his knuckles almost white from the force.

When Rose's mother opened the door, her expression changed from surprise to concern as she saw the look on Dave's face. She stepped back to let him in, her eyes filled with empathy and worry.

"Dave? Are you okay?" she asked, her voice filled with concern.

"No, I'm not," Dave replied, his voice trembling. "I think I'm going insane."

Rose's mother led him into the cozy living room, and they sat down together. Dave wasted no time in pouring out his heart, recounting every detail of his encounters. As he spoke, Rose's mother listened attentively, her gentle presence a source of comfort in his turmoil.

"Dave, your love for Rose is so strong, stronger than you realize," she said softly, taking his hand in hers. "It has consumed you, and that's why you're experiencing these feelings and visions."

Dave was taken aback. He didn't want to believe that he was hallucinating, but her words struck a chord. Could it be true? Could his grief be manifesting in such vivid ways? He looked at Rose's mother, searching for answers in her comforting gaze.

After a long conversation, Dave began to see things differently. He started to accept that perhaps his mind had been playing tricks on him, conjuring up images to cope with her loss.

It was a hard realization, but one that brought a strange sense of relief, knowing that he wasn't losing his mind.

"If Rose were still alive, even if she didn't show herself to you, I would know," Rose's mother said gently, seeing the conflict in Dave's eyes. "But she's not here, Dave. She's gone."

Dave repeated those words to himself, each time with a little more conviction. "Rose is gone," he whispered, finally accepting the painful truth. As he did, a sense of peace washed over him, knowing that Rose would always be a part of him, even if she was no longer physically by his side.

Dave stayed with Rose's family for a few days, despite his insistence on returning home to the island. Rose's mother was concerned about him being alone and made sure he was eating, noticing how much weight he had lost. She suggested that Dave sell the island, fearing it wasn't healthy for him to live there all alone without Rose. But Dave couldn't bear the thought of parting with the island, the place he and Rose had made their home together.

After saying his goodbyes and thanking Rose's family for their comfort, Dave left for the airport. Halfway there, he asked his driver to detour to the auction house where he first met Rose. He hadn't been able to go near it since her death, but now he felt ready. Sitting in the car, he gazed at the building's glass doors, remembering the night he met Rose. He felt paralyzed, unable to move or even open the car door. Just as he was about to tell his driver to continue on, a powerful feeling washed over him, giving him the strength to step out of the car and approach the building.

As Dave walked to the entrance, memories flooded his mind. He remembered the excitement he felt that night, the nervousness, and the instant connection he had with Rose. He pushed open the door, the familiar chime signaling his entrance. Inside, everything looked the same—the same layout, the same furniture. It was as if time had stood still since that fateful night.

Dave made his way to the spot where he would always find Rose, standing near a display of vintage jewelry. He touched the glass case, remembering how she had smiled at him, her eyes sparkling. The pain of her loss hit him afresh, and he felt tears welling up. But he also felt a sense of peace, as if being here had helped him in some way.

Dave returned to the car and instructed the driver to take him to the airport. His mind was filled with memories of his time with Rose, their laughter and love still fresh in his heart. Arriving at the airport, he asked the pilot to fly to Paris before returning to the island. The thought of being in the City of Love without Rose made his heart ache, but he knew he needed this time to reflect and heal.

Upon reaching Paris, there was enough time for a quick stop for some French fries and an apple galette. Dave found the bench near the Eiffel Tower, a place that held special memories for him and Rose. As he sat there, the tower began to sparkle, its lights dancing in the night sky. The sight was beautiful, but it only served to remind Dave of the emptiness he felt inside.

Sitting on the bench, Dave took a deep breath and began to eat, savoring the taste of the food but unable to shake the feeling of loneliness. He missed Rose more than ever in that moment, wishing she was there beside him to share in the beauty of the night.

Deciding to stay in Paris for the evening, Dave asked the hotel staff to empty the mini-fridge of all alcohol, determined to resist the temptation to drown his sorrows. Instead, he spent the rest of the evening lying in bed, staring out the window at the starlit sky. Several shooting stars streaked across the heavens, a sight that would have filled Rose with wonder. Dave closed his eyes and made a wish, wishing that somehow, somewhere, Rose could hear him: "I wish for a life free from pain and filled with happiness".

As Dave drifted into sleep that night, his mind slipped into a world where Rose was still alive, where they were together in the way he longed for. It felt so real, almost more tangible than waking life, as if his dreams were reality and reality a fleeting dream. For the first time since Rose's death, Dave slept a full night, cradled in the warmth of her presence, even if it was just in his mind.

In his dream, Rose's touch was soft and familiar, her voice a soothing melody that wrapped around him like a comforting blanket. They laughed together, danced under the stars, and shared whispered secrets as if they were the only two people in the world. It was a dream of pure bliss, a sanctuary from the harshness of his waking life.

When he awoke the next morning, the dream lingered like a sweet whisper in his ear. He replayed it in his mind, savoring every moment, finding solace in the fact that, even in his subconscious, Rose couldn't bear to be apart from him. It was a bittersweet comfort, a reminder of the deep love they shared.

As the day unfolded, Dave carried the dream with him, like a fragile treasure. It was a small respite from the ache of his loss, a fleeting glimpse of happiness in a world now dimmed by grief. Yet, even in that moment, he knew that no matter how much he tried to move forward, life without Rose would never be the same. She was woven into the fabric of his being, and without her, life felt incomplete, a puzzle missing its most vital piece.

But as the day wore on, the dream began to fade, slipping from his grasp like water through his fingers. The reality of Rose's absence hit him once again, a painful reminder that she was gone. He longed to return to the dream, to stay lost in its comfort forever, but he knew that he couldn't. He had to face the harshness of reality, to find a way to live in a world where Rose no longer existed. He knew that it would be filled with moments of longing and sadness, but he also knew that somewhere, deep within him, the memory of his dream would linger, a small piece of hope in the darkness of his grief.

Dave left the hotel and headed to the airport to make his way back home to the island. His pilots, as always, greeted him with respect, and together they took off. As the plane climbed into the sky, Dave's thoughts drifted to Rose. He missed her terribly, especially now, as he returned home without her by his side.

When Dave arrived back on the island, he took his private helicopter to the mainland to check the mail at the local post office, where he and Rose had a P.O. box. It was something he hadn't checked in many weeks. The post office clerk, a familiar face, greeted him warmly and handed over a large stack of letters and packages. There was so much mail that they had to store it in a separate bin in the back.

Dave took all the mail back home and slowly started going through it. Among the letters were a few undeliverable wedding invitations that had returned, which Dave couldn't bear to open to see the card inside. He tossed them into the fire that was burning in the living room fireplace, watching the flames consume them with a sense of finality.

After shuffling through many letters, Dave spotted one that was addressed to Rose from an address in Paris, addressing Rose as "Mon amour." Dave's heart skipped a beat. He was confused by this and opened the letter to read what was inside. What he found next broke his heart.

Inside the envelope, he found a letter from a man in Paris. It read, "Rose, my love, I hope this letter finds you. I didn't want to write to you, but my love for you overtook me, and I had to. I know you made the decision to move on and choose another man over me, but what we had could never be replaced. You may be happy, but I know you were happier with me. Please come back to me. I know our love is still strong."

Dave couldn't believe what he read. The letter was dated

the same day as the plane wreck. He had so many questions, as Rose had told Dave that she hadn't been in a relationship for years before she met Dave. He had so many questions but no one for answers. Dave noticed a return address, and his first thought was to go visit this mystery man. But he had just come back from Paris and was not sure how he would react once meeting this person. The letter had opened up a wound he thought was healing, and now he was faced with the reality that Rose might have kept secrets from him.

# Chapter Eleven

Dave found himself reading the letter over and over again. It was a crisp morning, the ocean breeze gently rustling the palm trees outside his window. The letter lay on his desk, its words a puzzle he couldn't solve. What could this letter mean? Was it true? Was this the man Dave had observed Rose with from behind the pay phone? His mind swirled with thoughts, memories of Rose flooding back with painful clarity. How would he react if Rose was still alive? How would he confront her? Did it still matter now that she was gone?

He read the letter again, his eyes scanning the words as if searching for hidden meaning. Why would she tell such a simple lie? Why claim she hadn't been in a relationship for several years before meeting him? It shouldn't have mattered; they weren't together at the time he saw them together, so why lie? Did she still have feelings for him but thought she couldn't tell Dave? He decided not to overreact. His love for Rose remained, and he missed her every day.

Dave put the letter in his safe, where it would stay for some time. Weeks passed, and Dave found himself restless, the silence of the island echoing his loneliness. He knew it was time to bring more people to the island, to breathe life back into its empty spaces. He felt a pang of guilt, as if by moving on, he was betraying the memory of Rose. But he knew she wouldn't want him to be alone, to wallow in grief forever.

He contacted all his contractors who had previously worked on the island's villas and resort, asking them to return to ensure everything was ready to welcome guests. Dave threw himself into the task, the busyness helping to numb the ache in his heart. He also reached out to agents to spread the word about the resort's reopening, wanting to share the beauty of the island with others.

It didn't take long, as when Dave and Rose first purchased the island, they had all repairs and remodeling completed. After just a few weeks, the island was fully staffed and stocked. Dave, for the first time since Rose's death, felt a slight feeling of excitement, something to look forward to.

Soon, it was opening day. News spread around the world that former Clark & Co. Owner Dave Clark had opened the island to the public. Soon after, the first bookings started to arrive at the island. Dave visited with many guests all over the island and welcomed them. The island was full of joy and smiles. Guests loved every inch of the resort; higher-end guests booked the villas and truly enjoyed it. Dave received great feedback from every guest that came to the island, and he enjoyed all the company that came through.

One evening, days after opening the island, as Dave was settling down for the day, there was a knock on the door, a knock so loud and urgent Dave thought there may have been a problem or even an emergency. Rushing to the door, he found no one there. As he took the first few steps, he noticed a familiar scent in the air. The scent was burned into his memory, a scent he had only smelled on one person before—Rose. It was the perfume that only he had ever smelled on her.

Dave glanced around, unsettled by the unexplained scent lingering in the air. With a cautious step, he retreated into the house, closing the door softly behind him. Standing just inches away from the door, he stared at it, his mind a blank slate.

Moments passed before he turned away, his steps echoing down the hallway, his thoughts still elusive. Suddenly, a wave of dizziness washed over him, forcing him to grip the wall for support. Amidst the haze, a familiar sound reached his ears—the beep of the answering machine in the kitchen. It was Rose's voice, asking, "Dave, can you hear me?" The same message he couldn't shake off as a mere accident.

Shock enveloped him. "What's going on?" he muttered, the message repeating relentlessly. Darting to the kitchen, the dizziness dissipating, Dave found the answering machine unplugged. A fallen book had dislodged the cord, leaving the machine silent. Holding the cord in disbelief, Dave stood frozen, trying to make sense of the inexplicable.

Dave's heart pounded in his chest as he tried to make sense of the situation. He replayed the message in his mind, each repetition only deepening his confusion. How could the answering machine play a message when it was clearly unplugged? It defied all logic.

Frustration and fear gnawed at him. He checked the phone line, searching for any sign of tampering or a hidden speaker. Everything appeared normal. He even checked the message again, just to be sure he hadn't imagined it. But there it was, Rose's voice, clear as day, asking if he could hear her.

Dave sank into a chair at the kitchen table, his mind racing. He thought of all the strange occurrences since the accident—the unexplained scents, the music playing on its own, and now this. Was it all in his head, a product of grief and stress? Or was there something more sinister at play?

He stared at the unplugged answering machine, a sense of unease settling over him. The rational part of his mind told him there had to be a logical explanation, but deep down, he couldn't shake the feeling that something was terribly wrong.

Dave retreated to the bedroom, his thoughts swirling like a tempest. He laid on the bed, staring at the ceiling, but sleep was elusive. The night passed in a haze of darkness and emptiness, devoid of dreams.

The following morning, Dave couldn't shake the events of the previous night from his mind. He decided to take action, starting by removing the answering machine from the house. Determined to find a path to healing, he made an appointment with a therapist.

The appointment was scheduled a few days out, and in the meantime, Dave was asked to journal his emotions and feelings to bring to the session. However, with the demands of managing the island and attending to the guests, he found it easier to record his thoughts rather than write them down.

His first recording began hesitantly. "It was day one, I have just lost the love of my life," he said, his voice breaking. Saying those words out loud overwhelmed him; he had spoken about Rose's loss but never with such finality. He spent the rest of the day engaging with guests and checking in with his staff, who had made the reopening of the island possible.

On the second day of recording, Dave admitted, "I feel a huge piece of myself and my life missing. I fear that I can't continue life without Rose." These words were followed by a long pause. He managed to record a few more thoughts, but it was a struggle, one of the hardest things he had ever done.

By the third day, the day before his therapy appointment, Dave's recordings took a different turn. "I feel as if Rose is still alive. I can feel her, and I think she is trying to communicate with me," he said, his voice filled with uncertainty. "I feel that she is lost, drifted onto the shore of a land that is unknown, lonely, and scared." These thoughts gave Dave pause. Was it possible that Rose was alive? Was their strong connection allowing her to communicate with him in some way?

The next morning, Dave packed his bags, preparing to head out to the mainland where he would stay for a few days. As he pulled clothes from the closet, the record player behind him suddenly started to play. It was Rose's favorite song, again. Dave froze, a shirt clenched tightly in his hand, and slowly turned around, his expression unreadable.

The music filled the room, surrounding Dave. How was this possible? He had already removed the record after the first time the song played by itself.

Feeling a surge of confusion and unease, Dave abandoned his packing, leaving his clothes strewn across the bed. Keeping his eyes fixed on the record player, he backed out of the room, the music haunting him every step of the way.

Without looking back, Dave hurried out of the house, leaving it unlocked, and made a beeline for his helicopter.

As Dave took off, he couldn't focus on flying, his mind swirling with confusion. His flight pattern had been erratic. Touching down at the airport, he powered down the helicopter and sat there, trying to make sense of what was happening. "Did I sleepwalk and replace the vinyl in the record player?" he wondered aloud, the words sounding absurd even to him. "But if I did, how did it start playing by itself?".

The questions echoed in his mind, each one pushing him further into a spiral of doubt. Was he losing his grip on reality? His therapy appointment was still several hours away, but he didn't know where else to go. He decided he would go straight to the therapist's office and wait.

As he sat there, lost in thought, the receptionist's voice cut through the haze. "Mr. Clark," she called out, her tone gentle but insistent. Dave didn't respond, his mind still far away. She tried again, moving closer and tapping him on the shoulder. "Mr. Clark," she repeated, her voice a little louder this time. Slowly, Dave came back to the present, his eyes meeting hers with a look of confusion and distress.

"The doctor is ready for your session," she informed him, her words a reminder of the reality he was trying to escape. Dave nodded, his movements mechanical as he followed her to the therapist's office. Sitting down, he tried to focus on the session ahead, but his mind kept drifting back to the unexplained events.

Throughout the session, Dave struggled to articulate his thoughts, the words catching in his throat. He felt as though he was teetering on the edge of a steep cliff, unsure of whether he would be able to find solid ground again.

As the session continued, Dave pulled out the recorder, a small device that he had faithfully used to voice record his thoughts and feelings over the last three days, as per the therapist's request. Pressing play, he expected to hear his innermost thoughts laid bare. Instead, there was only silence. Dave frowned, realizing that he must have forgotten to press record.

"I must have not pressed record," Dave said, a hint of frustration in his voice.

His therapist, a calm and attentive presence, listened as Dave recounted the unexplained occurrences that had haunted him since Rose's death. Each time, the therapist offered rational explanations, drawing on years of experience and psychological expertise. Dave listened, his skepticism slowly giving way to a reluctant acceptance of the therapist's reasoning.

"But why now? Why after all this time?" Dave asked, his voice betraying a hint of vulnerability.

The therapist smiled gently. "Grief doesn't follow a timeline, Dave. It comes in waves, sometimes when we least expect it."

As the session drew to a close, Dave felt a weight lift off his shoulders. Perhaps there was an explanation for everything, even if he couldn't understand it fully. He left the therapist's office with a newfound sense of clarity, ready to face the challenges ahead with a renewed perspective.

Walking out into the crisp evening air, Dave couldn't shake the feeling that maybe, just maybe, there was a logical explanation for everything that had happened. And perhaps, in time, he would come to understand it all.

Over the next several months, Dave continued his therapy sessions, immersing himself in the process of healing. He found peace in the routine, spending extended periods on the mainland, only returning to his island home to collect clothing and to oversee the resort and his staff. Each session brought him closer to a sense of normalcy, a gradual reawakening of his spirit.

As time passed, Dave noticed a shift within himself. The darkness that had clouded his thoughts began to dissipate, replaced with hope. He dared to believe that life was finally coming back together, that he could start anew with a fresh perspective.

For months, Dave experienced no more unexplained encounters, and he allowed himself to relax, thinking, "Everything is getting better." He embraced the notion that perhaps the worst was behind him, that he was on the path to recovery.

However, one evening, after going to bed, a strange sensation crept over him, a feeling of unease that he couldn't shake.

# Chapter Twelve

That night, Dave made a decision that would change everything. He reached for the bottle of buspirone, a medication his therapist had prescribed to help ease the anxiety that had gripped him since Rose's death. After swallowing a pill, he felt a calming wave wash over him, his mind clearing, and the weight on his chest easing.

He laid in bed, watching mindless TV to distract himself until sleep mercifully took him. But his rest was short-lived. In the dead of night, Dave was startled awake by what felt like the tightest hug imaginable and the unmistakable sound of Rose's voice calling out to him, "Dave, wake up. I need you."

His heart racing, Dave shot out of bed, his mind racing with a mix of fear and hope. Could it be possible? "Where are you?" Dave called out into the darkness, desperate for a sign. But there was only silence, and no matter how hard he tried, sleep eluded him for the rest of the night.

The next morning, Dave sat up in his bed, staring off into the room. For hours, he just sat there, his mind empty, not a single thought crossing it. Dave was beaten down. Losing his wife in a plane wreck, the signs of Rose haunting him, and the letter from the man who may have had a part of Rose's heart completely destroyed him.

After hours, Dave decided that he was going to find this mystery man to find out the truth. He didn't know how he would react, but he had the address of the sender, and that's where he would start. With no time to waste, Dave called his pilots to prep the plane for a trip to Paris. Later that evening, Dave met the pilots, and they took off.

On the flight, Dave found it easier to fall asleep, comforted by the presence of familiar faces on the private plane. Despite his nervousness about uncovering the truth behind the mysterious man in the letter, Dave eventually drifted off into sleep.

Hours later, Dave was abruptly awakened by the sound of Rose's voice, pleading with him not to go. Her words were clear and vivid, as though she were right beside him, whispering in his ear. Wide awake now, Dave couldn't dismiss what he had heard as a figment of his imagination. It felt like a message from beyond, a sign from Rose herself.

"What do you mean, 'don't go'? To Paris?" Dave whispered into the quiet cabin. Was Rose warning him not to pursue the truth, fearing it would only bring him more pain? Dave was torn, unsure of whether to heed her supposed warning or to continue on his quest to Paris, in search of the man who may have been a lover of his late wife. Ultimately, Dave chose to press on. Upon arriving in Paris several hours later, he found the city engulfed in a late-night storm. Opting to wait out the weather, Dave checked into a hotel for the evening, determined to unravel the mystery that lay ahead.

The next morning, Dave called for his driver to take him to the address on the letter. It was not far from his hotel, only a 15-

minute drive. As they drove, the early morning sunlight filtered through the windows, casting a warm glow over the city streets. Dave stared out at the passing scenery, his mind preoccupied with thoughts of what awaited him at the mysterious address.

Suddenly, a sharp pain pierced through his temples, causing him to wince. It felt as though a thousand tiny needles were pricking at his brain. He winced, placing a hand to his forehead, hoping to alleviate the pain. But it only seemed to intensify, spreading like wildfire through his head.

"Stop the car," Dave finally managed to croak out, his voice strained. The driver, alarmed by the sudden request, quickly pulled over to the side of the road. Dave stumbled out of the car, his head spinning, and he collapsed onto the back seat, hoping that lying down would ease the pain.

As he lay there, his eyes closed tightly shut, the pain only seemed to worsen. It was then that he felt it – a series of sharp, electric shocks coursing through his chest. His body convulsed with each shock, and he could do nothing but grit his teeth and endure the agony.

After what felt like an eternity, the pain subsided, leaving Dave gasping for air. He opened his eyes, blinking away the tears that had welled up from the pain. He knew this wasn't a heart attack – it felt different, more intense, and more frightening.

Slowly, Dave sat up, his breathing still ragged. He stepped out of the car, his legs feeling like jelly beneath him. The cool morning air helped to clear his head, and he took a few deep breaths, trying to steady himself.

The driver, concerned, asked Dave if he was okay, but Dave could only nod weakly, not wanting to worry the man further. He knew he had to continue to the address on the letter, despite the ordeal he had just experienced. With a deep breath, he climbed back into the car, determined to uncover the secrets that lay ahead.

After a few moments, they arrived at the destination. Dave sat in the car for a few minutes, trying to gather himself after the painful encounter he had just experienced. He closed his eyes, taking deep breaths to calm his racing heart. Memories of Rose flooded his mind, and he could still hear her voice echoing in his ears.

Finally, Dave opened his eyes and got out of the car. He stood for a moment, leaning against the door, steeling himself for what was to come. He needed to be strong, to find out the truth, no matter how difficult it might be.

He walked towards the front door, his footsteps heavy with emotion. When he reached the door, he raised his hand to knock, but hesitated. The sound of laughter from inside gave him pause. He could hear the happiness in their voices, and for a moment, he considered turning back. He didn't want to intrude on their joy, to disrupt their lives.

But then, a wave of anger washed over him. He had been through too much to walk away now. He needed answers, closure. With a deep breath, he knocked on the door, his heart pounding in his chest.

Right before he could knock again, the door creaked open, revealing a man with a warm smile. "Puis-je vous aider?" he asked in French. Dave's grasp of French was tenuous, but he understood enough. He inquired about English, and the man nodded, "I do."

Dave stood there, momentarily speechless, as if the words had fled his mind, staring at the man. Then, a memory rushed back— the day he had seen Rose with this man, who had kissed her on the cheeks while he hid behind the phone booth. Rose had mentioned him as a French client. "It's you," Dave finally uttered, realization dawning, "you are the man I saw her with, the man who wrote the letter."

The man looked puzzled at first, but then recognition

dawned. "You are Rose's husband," he stated in French, his smile fading.

"I cannot speak with you here," the man continued, glancing around cautiously. He instructed Dave to meet him at a bench near the Eiffel Tower—the very bench Dave and Rose had frequented, watching the twinkling lights at dawn.

Dave couldn't believe it. He was in shock. Why would he choose the same bench, the bench that Dave always sat on and later shared with Rose? "Did Rose meet with him at the same bench?" Dave began to think. Lost in his mind, the entire drive to the tower, he just stared into space, lost in his thoughts, pondering every scenario, and they kept getting worse. "Did she continue seeing him after we got together?" "Was it all a lie?" Dave couldn't stop thinking that Rose had been in a relationship with this man that continued after they started seeing each other. His mind was eating him alive, but in this moment, he began to miss Rose even more. Not only because he wanted answers, but he needed her comfort, the comfort that she gave him that always eased his worries and pain.

In that moment, he felt a sensation, the same that awoke him in his sleep not too long ago, the feeling of Rose's touch, the feeling of being hugged, hands rubbing over his forehead. With his head laid back in the seat of the car, his eyes closed, feeling paralyzed, he again heard her voice once more, "I cannot live without you." Dave replied softly, "I won't live without you," as tears ran down his face.

The car pulled up near the Eiffel Tower, and Dave spotted the man already seated on the bench, waiting for their meeting. Dave approached slowly, settling down beside him without a word, his gaze fixed ahead. After a few moments of silence, Dave turned to the man. "Who are you?" he asked, his voice barely above a whisper.

The man, named Alain, turned to face Dave. "I first want to tell you how sorry I am for the loss of your wife," he began, his tone sincere. "I, too, am in pain."

Dave was taken aback. "In pain?" he repeated, confusion evident in his voice. "Why are you in pain? How do you know my wife? And why did you write her that letter?"

Alain looked out towards the iconic tower, cradling a steaming cup of coffee in his hands. "Rose and I were lovers many years ago," he revealed softly. "I loved her with all of my heart. I was obsessed."

Dave's heart began to race, a mix of emotions swirling within him. Before he could respond, Alain continued, his voice tinged with sorrow. "We drifted apart. We no longer shared the same interests, and one evening, she left. But I know she always still loved me."

Dave sat in stunned silence, the weight of Alain's words settling heavily upon him. The revelation about Rose's past with Alain opened a floodgate of questions and emotions.

Dave wanted to ask so many questions, about the day he saw Alain and Rose together but his heart couldn't take any more pain. Dave stood up and walked away, leaving Alain sitting on the bench. Alain did not say a word and stayed behind as Dave got into his vehicle and instructed his driver to take him back to the hotel.

After returning, Dave found himself in front of the mini fridge, stocked with alcohol. He had promised both himself and Rose that he would never drink again, and he had kept that promise even after her passing. But on this night, the weight of his grief bore down on him, and he found himself reaching for a bottle, then another, until the room spun and he succumbed to the numbing embrace of alcohol, drinking himself into a stupor.

In his drunken haze, Dave slipped into a deep sleep, one that felt more like a haunting than a dream. It was a vivid replay of the plane crash, but with a surreal twist. The dream began at the airport, with Rose waiting for him, radiant as ever, but this time she was cradling a baby girl in her arms. Confusion etched on his face, Dave approached her, and she simply said, "Your baby needs you," offering the child to him.

Dave took the baby, and the weight of the infant in his arms felt astonishingly real, as if this were truly his child. The dream then shifted to mid-flight, with Dave and Rose seated, she gently rocking the baby to sleep. As the plane descended and eventually crashed into the ocean, the dream diverged from reality once more. Dave found himself sinking into the depths, in silence, watching the flames from the wreckage fade into the darkness as he sank deeper, with Rose desperately swimming after him, her hand outstretched but never quite reaching him.

He watched as the light dimmed, until there was only darkness. And then, everything was still. When Dave woke up the next morning, everything seemed different. The emotions he felt, the thoughts swirling in his mind, the grief weighing heavy on his heart—it all felt altered. Dave felt numb, questioning the purpose of life and whether it was worth continuing.

Later that day, Dave called for his private plane to be fueled and prepared for departure back to his island home. As he headed to the airport, he noticed a change in the atmosphere.

Once returning home the island seemed deserted; the resort devoid of any signs of life. There were no employees, no guests—everything appeared untouched, as if it had never been inhabited.

Dave's heart sank. "Was it all a figment of my imagination?" he wondered. "Did I never open the resort and simply imagine its existence?" Confusion consumed Dave as he wandered from building to building, finding no evidence of human presence.

Uncertain of what to do, Dave called his therapist for guidance, only to discover that he was not a patient at that clinic. Dave felt like he was losing touch with reality, his sense of self slipping away.

Returning home, Dave noticed the answering machine, which he had previously removed, was back, with a blinking light indicating a message. With hesitation, he pressed play and heard a message that shook him to the core.

"Hey, this is us from the past, on our way home," the message began. "Dave, say something." "Hey, future me, you're now married to the most beautiful person in the world. Treat her with love, respect, and make her your priority for life. See you soon."

Dave was stunned. He had removed the answering machine, and the message was not the original one he had heard. As a searing pain shot through his chest and his head throbbed relentlessly, he collapsed to the ground, hearing Rose's voice cry out, "Dave, no!" just before losing consciousness.

# Chapter Thirteen

Dave's memories started to consume him , pulling him back to moments etched deeply into his past. It all began when he was just a young boy, a mere school kid waiting for a ride home. Dave would sit on the steps of his school, his backpack slouched beside him, eyes scanning the road for his father's car. He knew his father would be late, always stopping at the liquor store before picking him up. It was like watching a movie from the sidelines, observing himself as a child, waiting in anticipation.

Then, the memory shifts to a darker scene, the day his father died. The phone call that shattered their world, informing them of the fatal wreck caused by his father's intoxicated state. Dave vividly remembers the moment when he and his mother, Dee, received the news. His mother's anguished cry as she collapsed to the floor, the phone slipping from her grasp, dangling on its cord. Dave, frozen in shock and disbelief, sees the reflection of his own face in the mirror of his memory, a stark reminder of the past that haunts him.

As Dave's memory shifted again, it was like watching clips of a movie, each scene a haunting reminder of his past.

The next scene was of the day the local sheriff and child services came to his home. Dave saw his mother sitting on the couch, her face blank with shock, as the sheriff spoke to her. She held a blanket tightly, perhaps seeking comfort in its fabric. The sheriff explained that they would be taking Dave away. The image shifted, and Dave witnessed child services pulling him out of his home, right past his mother. He screamed and cried for her, but she remained silent, seemingly unaware of what was happening.

The scene after flashed to the days in state custody, where Dave awaited his mother's return. But that day never came. He watched his younger self writing countless letters, pleading to come back home, each word a desperate cry for the comfort and security of his mother's embrace. The nights were long and sleepless, filled with tears and worries that he would never see her again.

Then came the memory of his mother's death. Dave watched himself as a child, crying inconsolably for his mother. Suddenly, there was a knock on the door behind him. The same sheriff who had taken him away from his mother stepped through the door, passing through Dave as if he were a ghost. The sheriff explained to the younger Dave that his mother had taken her own life.

Through it all, Dave stood as a silent observer, a ghost from his past, watching these painful memories flood back with a clarity that was both agonizing and cathartic.

As each memory flashed before Dave's eyes, they seemed to blur together, a rapid montage of moments from his life. Step by step, moment by moment, he relived it all, from his earliest days to the present. Yet, amidst this torrent of memories, he felt nothing —no sadness, no anger, just a detached observation.

Then, in a sudden burst of light, the memories stood still, and Dave found himself standing in front of the auction house, back to the day he first met Rose. He watched himself, a ghostly observer, as he frantically searched for his forgotten Birkin bag. And then, there she was—Rose. Dave's heart skipped a beat as he watched himself notice her for the first time.

Even as a ghost, a dream, or whatever this experience was, Dave felt a surge of emotion unlike anything he had ever felt. It was love, pure and overwhelming. Watching Rose, these memories felt as vivid as real life, and for the first time since her passing, he felt a deep connection to her.

Past Dave was speechless, struck by an instant and profound love for Rose. And as Dave watched, tears streamed down his cheeks, sadness washing over him. It was a feeling he had not experienced since this strange journey through his memories began.

Dave walked up to Rose, his hand reaching for hers, but instead of touching her, it all shifted once more.

The next memory led him to a day when he saw Rose while driving down the road. Ghostly Dave stood on the sidewalk, watching himself jump out of the vehicle that had not yet come to a complete stop. He power-walked towards Rose, excitement written all over his face. But then, his excitement turned to disappointment as he saw Rose hug and kiss another man. Dave, now observing from beside himself hiding behind a phone booth, whispered in his own ear, "You will make the most amazing memories with her, you are the lucky one." And in that moment, the memories once again shifted to the next.

The scene changed once again, and Dave found himself back to the day he had his heart attack. He watched himself lay in the streets as a homeless man began CPR on him. The ambulance rushed to his rescue, the doctors worked on him to bring him back to life, and then there was darkness. Present Dave realized that this was when he fell into the hypoxic coma.

Then, something new appeared in his memories, something that was not part of his conscious memory. Dave saw Rose sitting by the side of his bed, a few days before he first saw her at the hospital, before the knock at the door when he first saw her come into the room. Rose was by his side before she truly was by his side. Dave couldn't believe it. "This can't be true," he thought. How could all these other memories be so accurate, and yet this one wrong?

Dave knew these flashbacks of memories could not be a dream; they were too real. He also knew that he was not asleep. He had free will of thoughts, movement, and now, emotions. "Am I dead?" Dave whispered. "Am I seeing my life flash before me, all of reality?"

Dave floated through his memories. He watched his first date with Rose, the nervous excitement he felt when he saw her, the way her eyes sparkled when she smiled. He saw himself proposing to her, the ring glittering in his hand as he professed his love.

The memories continued, a montage of their life together. Days spent at auctions, Rose always finding the perfect pieces for his jewelry empire. The adventures they embarked on, exploring new places and creating cherished memories. The day they decided to buy the island and make it their home, dreaming of a future filled with happiness.

But not all memories were happy. There were moments of pain and loss. The day Rose had a miscarriage, the grief and emptiness that followed. The day she returned home to Spain, leaving Dave behind. The loneliness that consumed him, the feeling of being adrift without her by his side.

And then there was the darkest moment, the day he walked into the open waters of the ocean, desperate to end his pain. The memory was raw and painful, a reminder of how close he had come to losing everything.

But amidst the darkness, there were moments of light. The joy of moving forward with their wedding plans, the bliss of their honeymoon in Bora Bora. Dave held onto these memories, the moments of happiness and love that sustained him.

As the memories continued to unfold, Dave couldn't help but feel a sense of unease. Was he stuck in this loop of memories, doomed to relive them over and over again? Would they consume him, leaving nothing but a shell of who he once was?

Everything slowed down as a new memory emerged, one that would change everything. He saw himself at the airport, the same airport where he and Rose had departed on that fateful day. The day that changed his life forever, the day that led him to this moment, the moment he was currently experiencing.

Dave watched as he and Rose boarded the plane, their steps light with the excitement of their honeymoon. He stood beside their seats, invisible yet present, a ghost in his own past. The love between them was palpable, their laughter and conversation filling the air with warmth.

Again, he heard the captain's voice over the intercom, announcing a faulty sensor that needed repairs. Dave knew it would take hours, but he didn't mind. For him, this memory was a treasure, a chance to be with Rose again, if only as a silent observer.

As time passed in the memory, Dave remained, watching them talk and laugh, feeling a bittersweet comfort in their presence. He knelt beside Rose, pressing a ghostly kiss to her cheek, wishing she could feel it. She turned slightly, almost as if she sensed him, but in reality, she was scanning the cabin, unaware of his presence.

Hours slipped by, the captain's voice finally announcing that the plane was ready for takeoff. Dave felt a pang of unease, knowing what lay ahead. He didn't want to relive the crash, the pain and loss that would follow. He watched helplessly as the plane taxied down the runway, his heart heavy with the weight of what was to come.

As the plane ascended into the sky, Dave's anxiety grew. He remembered the sudden jolt, the screams of passengers, and the feeling of weightlessness as the plane started to lose control. He clenched his fists, unable to change the course of events, knowing that in a few moments, their lives would change forever.

Dave felt a profound sense of helplessness. The plane's descent toward the ocean, with Rose clinging to him in fear, was a moment frozen in time. Everything seemed to slow down, stretching the few seconds before impact into an agonizing eternity. The crash, when it finally came, was both sudden and painfully slow, the plane breaking apart as it hit the water, sending a shiver down Dave's spine.

In this surreal state, Dave's perspective shifted. No longer just an observer, he was now a part of the scene, submerged in the dark abyss. The wreckage above cast eerie shadows, and the flames flickered, illuminating the underwater world before slowly fading away. Through the murky water, he saw Rose swimming towards him, her hand outstretched, her face a mix of determination and desperation. This was not how Dave remembered, yet he had dreamt this just prior to all of these memories.

Then, everything went dark. No more memories followed, only an endless void. In the darkness, Dave felt a strange sensation, as if his body was there but unable to move, trapped in the blackness. It was then that he heard Rose's voice, a soft whisper cutting through the emptiness.

"Baby, you've been so strong through all of this," her voice filled with love and sorrow. "I have prayed for you day and night, watched over you. You are my everything. You've been my hero, my rock. You've taught me strength when I was weak, been by my side through it all. I know you can't feel your pain, but I feel mine. I will show Lilly the world, make her know you and who you were. We will be okay. You can let go. I love you!"

With those words, Dave was swallowed by darkness, drifting into an eternal slumber. He was surrounded by memories of his past and the promise of a future he would never see.

# Chapter Fourteen

Suddenly, the plane crashed into the South Pacific Ocean....

As the plane hit the water, Rose held onto Dave's hand until the moment of impact and for a few moments after. But then, she felt his hand being pulled away from hers. Despite this, she never lost sight of him. Dave was unconscious and began to sink deeper into the ocean's embrace.

Rose swam after him, diving as deep as she could with barely any air in her lungs. She pushed herself to the limit, but Dave continued to sink further out of reach. With no air left in her lungs, she knew she had to return to the surface, but she couldn't bear the thought of losing him.

Determined to save Dave, Rose made one last desperate effort. She stretched her hand out as far as she could, and just as she was about to turn back, her fingers brushed against his. With a surge of adrenaline, she grasped his hand tightly and kicked her feet as hard as she could, propelling them both back to the surface.

Gasping for air, Rose knew that time was running out for Dave. She began to perform CPR right there in the water, alternating between chest compressions and breaths into his mouth, all while screaming for help. She was determined to keep him alive, even against the overwhelming odds.

Just as Rose lost all hope a bright light from above struck her, it was a search and rescue helicopter. Rose with all the power she had left in her screamed as loud as she could waving her hands while she was holding onto Dave not letting go again.

A few moments later, a diver bravely leaped from the hovering helicopter, a rescue basket swinging beneath him. With precision, Dave was carefully lifted into the basket and hoisted up to the waiting aircraft, followed by Rose. Despite the urgency of their situation, Dave remained unconscious, prompting the medic aboard the helicopter to immediately initiate life-saving procedures. Throughout the tense flight back to the mainland, the medic tirelessly worked to revive Dave. Miraculously, Dave began spitting up water, a sign of hope, and briefly opened his eyes before slipping back into unconsciousness.

Rose clung to this glimmer of hope as they arrived at the crash site's recovery zone, where Dave was swiftly transferred to another helicopter bound for a nearby hospital. Upon their arrival, Dave was rushed into the care of a team of doctors who began an intensive effort to save his life.

After hours of frantic efforts, the lead doctor emerged and sat down with Rose, who sat anxiously, her hands tightly clasped. With gentle compassion, the doctor explained the devastating news, "I'm sorry to have to tell you this, but your husband, Dave, has suffered from an anoxic brain injury." The doctor went on to explain the nature of this injury, which occurs when the brain is deprived of oxygen for an extended period, as in near-drowning incidents. The prognosis was grim; the damage to Dave's brain was severe, and his chances of recovery were uncertain. The doctor outlined the potential long-term effects, including cognitive impairments, motor deficits, and the possibility of a persistent vegetative state. As Rose absorbed the weight of these words, the reality of Dave's condition began to sink in, leaving her heart heavy with despair.

Rose asked to see Dave, her need to be with him overwhelming. Understanding the importance of her presence, the doctor allowed Rose to stay by Dave's side, knowing that time was now the critical factor. Only time would determine Dave's fate, and Rose was determined to be there for every moment of it, holding onto hope and love as her unwavering companions.

When Rose entered the room, tears streamed down her face, and she fell onto Dave in disbelief. A few moments later, the door behind her opened, and another doctor entered the room. "Hello, I am Dr. Aline," he announced calmly, "I will be the primary doctor taking over Dave's care Rose did not acknowledge the doctor; she continued to stay by Dave's side, her head resting on his chest.

The rest of that day, Rose lay by Dave's side, her tears the only sound breaking the heavy silence of the room. She prayed fervently for him to wake up, reminiscing about the good times they shared and making promises of the future they would build together once he regained consciousness. Still in shock and feeling utterly alone, Rose couldn't bring herself to call her family yet; all she wanted was to be with Dave.

The next day, Rose woke up beside Dave, still without any new answers. The doctor was scheduled to come in late morning for more scans, but there seemed to be no signs of improvement. When the doctor arrived, Dave was taken for a full-body scan, as the initial examination upon admission had focused on immediate life-threatening injuries. After several hours, Dave was returned to his room, where Rose anxiously awaited.

Dr. Aline entered the room and discussed their findings with Rose. "Dave has two broken ribs, a fractured ankle, and a severely sprained wrist," the doctor informed her. "But our biggest concern is whether he will wake up from the coma and, if he does, the extent of the brain damage." After thanking the doctor, Rose turned back to Dave, overwhelmed with guilt. "Why did I escape without a scratch, but you're facing all of this?" she whispered to him, laying her had gently back on his chest.

Later that evening, Rose decided to play music for Dave, hoping to stimulate his mind if he could hear his surroundings. She chose her favorite song, the one they would listen to almost every morning in their home. She played this song several times a day, hoping it would help bring him back.

As the music played, Rose gently took off her ring and placed it in Dave's hand, closing his fingers around it. Leaning in close, she whispered, "Can you hear me?" In that moment, she noticed a slight movement in Dave's eye, which she interpreted as a sign of acknowledgment, even though the doctors had cautioned her that he might have involuntary eye movements.

Many days passed with no signs of improvement in Dave's condition. Despite her reluctance to leave his side, Rose knew she needed a break. She decided to go for a walk to get some fresh air and find something to eat. She had been by Dave's side non-stop since the accident, eating very little and mostly from the hospital cafeteria. Still dressed in the clothes she wore since leaving Bora Bora, she made her way to the hospital gift shop to purchase some fresh clothing—a basic t-shirt and some shorts. Afterward, she took a refreshing shower at the hospital before stepping out to get some fresh food and clear her mind.

Returning to Dave's room after her shower, Rose gave him a tight hug and a kiss on the forehead, reassuring him that she would be back soon. "I won't be gone long," she whispered to him as he lay with his eyes closed, appearing deeply asleep.

As she turned to leave, her mother and sister Sofia walked through the door. They ran towards Rose, giving her a tight hug, tears of joy streaming down their faces at her survival of the crash. Rose was overwhelmed with emotion at the sight of her family, grateful for their presence during this difficult time.

After a long hug, Roses mother walked up to Dave, her

hand resting on his forehead as she prayed in Spanish: "Señor Todopoderoso, te pedimos que cures a nuestro ser querido, un hombre valiente, que se encuentra en coma. Con tu poder divino, sana su cuerpo y su espíritu, y permite que despierte y vuelva a nosotros. Te pedimos humildemente que guíes a los médicos y enfermeras que lo cuidan, para que puedan brindarle el mejor tratamiento posible. Confiamos en tu bondad y misericordia, y te agradecemos por escuchar nuestras oraciones. Amén."

Translated, her prayer meant: "Almighty Lord, we ask you to heal our loved one, a brave man, who is in a coma. With your divine power, heal his body and spirit, and allow him to wake up and return to us. We humbly ask you to guide the doctors and nurses who care for him, so they can provide the best possible treatment. We trust in your kindness and mercy, and we thank you for hearing our prayers. Amen."

Afterwards, she took his hand and kissed it, standing there for a few moments while Sofia held Rose in the back of the Room.

Together, Rose, her mother, and Sofia left the room and headed for town. It was a relief for Rose to step outside the hospital walls, to feel the warmth of the sun on her skin and the gentle breeze in her hair. The streets were bustling with life, a stark contrast to the somber atmosphere of the hospital.

They walked in silence for a while, each lost in their own thoughts. Rose felt a sense of peace being surrounded by her loved ones, grateful for their support. As they passed by a small café, Rose's stomach growled, reminding her that she had barely eaten anything substantial since the accident.

They decided to stop and have a meal, sitting at a table

outside. Rose savored each bite, the food tasting better than she could remember. Her mother and Sofia watched her with concern, knowing how difficult this time had been for her.

After their meal, they wandered through the streets, browsing in shops and taking in the sights. Rose felt a sense of normalcy returning, a glimmer of hope amidst the uncertainty of Dave's condition.

As they walked, Rose noticed a small church up ahead. A feeling of peace washed over her, and she suggested they go inside. The church was quiet, the only sound the soft shuffle of their feet on the stone floor. Rose lit a candle and knelt in prayer, her heart heavy with worry for Dave but also filled with hope.

After spending some time in prayer, they left the church and continued their stroll through the town. As they passed a flower shop, Rose's mother suggested they buy some flowers for Dave. They carefully selected a bouquet of his favorite flowers and headed back to the hospital.

Upon their return, they went straight to Dave's room. Rose placed the flowers on the bedside table, arranging them carefully. She sat by Dave's side, holding his hand and talking to him softly, updating him on their day and the town they had explored.

As the evening drew near, Rose's mother and Sofia reluctantly said their goodbyes, promising to return the next day. Rose watched them leave, feeling grateful for their visit and the strength they had given her.

Alone with Dave once more, Rose settled in for the night. She whispered words of love and encouragement, knowing that somewhere deep inside him, Dave could hear her. She fell asleep by his side, her hand resting in his, holding onto hope for his recovery.

# Chapter Fifteen

As Rose settled back into the quiet rhythm of the hospital room, the evening light fading through the window, she reflected on the past few days. They had been a whirlwind of emotions and unexpected challenges, yet through it all, Rose felt a deep connection to Dave, as if their bond was being tested and strengthened in ways she had never imagined.

That night, as Rose lay beside Dave, her mind raced with worries and what-ifs. She felt an unusual queasiness, a sensation she initially attributed to stress and exhaustion. However, as the night wore on, the feeling intensified, and she found herself rushing to the bathroom multiple times, each episode leaving her weaker and more puzzled about the cause.

The following morning, with Dave still in the same unresponsive state, Rose felt a wave of exhaustion wash over her as she tried to stand up from her makeshift bed next to his. Her legs felt shaky, and a sudden dizziness overwhelmed her. Clutching the edge of Dave's bed for support, Rose's vision blurred momentarily, and then darkness engulfed her as she fainted, collapsing onto the floor.

The commotion caught the attention of a passing nurse, who quickly assessed the situation and called for immediate assistance. Medical staff hurried into the room, and Rose was gently lifted onto a stretcher and taken to an examination room for evaluation.

As Rose lay in the examination room, drifting in and out of consciousness, she heard snippets of conversation about her condition. "Possible dehydration... stress... we need to run some tests," the voices said, a mixture of concern and clinical detachment filling the air.

Hours passed, and Rose slowly regained consciousness, her mother and Sofia by her side, their faces etched with worry. The doctor finally entered, a clipboard in hand, and addressed Rose gently. "We've run some tests, and while you're certainly dealing with dehydration and exhaustion, there's another reason for your symptoms," the doctor paused, checking her notes. "Rose, you're pregnant."

The room fell silent as the weight of the words hung in the air. Rose's eyes widened in shock, her hand instinctively moving to her stomach. A flurry of emotions cascaded through her—joy, fear, disbelief. The reality of being pregnant, especially under such dire circumstances, was overwhelming.

"Given your current condition and the stress you've been under, we need to monitor you closely," the doctor continued, her tone reassuring. "We'll take good care of you and the baby."

Rose nodded, still processing the news. As she was wheeled back to Dave's room, her mind raced with thoughts of their future child. A bittersweet feeling overtook her; joy for the new life growing inside her mingled with sorrow for Dave's uncertain fate.

Back by Dave's side, Rose took his hand, her touch gentle. She leaned in close, whispering the news to him. "Dave, we're going to have a baby," she said softly, her voice filled with a mixture of hope and sadness. "You have to come back to us."

The days that followed were a delicate balance of caring for herself and being there for Dave. Rose made sure to eat properly and rest when needed, all the while keeping her vigil by Dave's side. Her mother and Sofia were constant presences, offering support and taking care of her when she couldn't.

One evening, as Rose sat beside Dave, a gentle melody filled the room. It was the song, the one that had been a constant throughout their relationship. Rose felt a small movement from Dave's hand—a slight squeeze. Tears filled her eyes as she looked at him, a glimmer of hope sparking within her.

"Keep fighting, Dave," she whispered, her voice steady but full of emotion. "We need you."

As night fell, Rose continued to hold Dave's hand, the soft beeping of the hospital machines a constant backdrop. She drifted to sleep, dreams mixing with reality, a deep, unshakeable faith holding her steady. She believed in miracles, and now, more than ever, she needed one.

The gentle hum of the hospital machinery had become a familiar, albeit unsettling, background noise to Rose as she maintained her constant vigil by Dave's side. The rhythmic beeping of the heart monitor was oddly comforting in its consistency. However, late one evening, as the hospital lobby quieted down and the dim lights cast long shadows across the room, the comforting rhythm suddenly changed. The steady beeps turned into a high-pitched, continuous tone, signaling an emergency.

Rose's heart raced as she leapt to her feet, her hands trembling as she pressed the emergency button frantically. Within moments, the room was flooded with medical staff, their movements swift and their faces set in grim determination. The lead nurse quickly assessed the situation and barked orders to the team. "We're losing him," she said urgently. "Prepare for immediate resuscitation."

Dave's heart had stopped.

Rose was gently but firmly guided out of the room as the medical team began their life-saving efforts. The lobby felt cold and empty as she leaned against the wall, her knees weak. Tears streamed down her face as she whispered prayers, begging for Dave to pull through.

After what felt like an eternity, the doctor emerged, his expression somber. "Rose, Dave's heart stopped due to a complication from his previous injuries and his current condition. We need to perform emergency surgery right now to address a blood clot that has formed near his heart. It's risky, but it's his only chance."

Rose nodded, unable to speak, her mind reeling from the sudden turn of events. She signed the necessary consent forms through blurred vision, her signature shaky but determined.

As Dave was rushed to the operating room, Rose sank into a chair in the waiting area. Her mother and Sofia arrived soon after, having been called by the hospital staff. They sat beside her, offering silent support, each lost in their own worried thoughts.

The hours during the surgery were agonizing. Rose felt every minute stretch into an eternity, her heart heavy with fear and hope. Finally, the surgeon emerged, looking weary but cautiously optimistic. "The surgery went as well as we could have hoped," he explained. "We were able to remove the clot and stabilize his heart, but the next 48 hours are critical. He's still very weak, and we need to monitor him closely."

Relief washed over Rose, mixed with an enduring sense of fear. She thanked the surgeon, her voice hoarse from worry and fatigue, and was soon allowed to see Dave. He was back in the ICU, surrounded by machines and tubes, more fragile than ever.

Rose took her usual place by his side, her hand finding his. The room was quiet, save for the soft beeping of the monitors. She spoke to him softly, telling him about the baby, their plans, and her love for him. Each word was a pledge, a promise to stay by his side.

As days turned into weeks, there were small victories and significant setbacks. Dave remained in a coma, his condition stable but critical. Rose kept her routine, dividing her time between caring for herself and being with Dave. Her pregnancy was progressing, and with it came a mix of emotions—joy at the life growing inside her, and sorrow at experiencing it without Dave awake by her side.

One morning, as Rose sat by Dave, the doctor came in with an update. "His condition is stable, but we're not seeing the improvement we hoped for," he said gently. "It's still a waiting game, Rose. I'm sorry there isn't more we can do right now."

Rose nodded, her gaze fixed on Dave. "I understand. Thank you for everything," she replied, her voice steady despite the turmoil inside her.

The hospital became a world of its own, with days blending into nights. Rose found comfort in small routines—talking to Dave, playing their favorite music, and reading books aloud. She would often place his hand on her growing belly, hoping he could feel the baby move.

Then, one late afternoon, as Rose was leaving the cafeteria with a cup of tea, her phone rang. It was the hospital. Heart pounding, she rushed back to Dave's room, fearing the worst.

When she arrived, she found the room bustling with activity. The nurses were adjusting equipment, and the doctor met her at the door. "Rose, Dave's condition has changed," he said urgently. "We've noticed some reflex movements, a good sign, but his heart rate is fluctuating. We need to keep a close eye on him."

Encouraged yet frightened, Rose spent the night by Dave's side, watching every slight movement, every change in the monitors.

The next morning brought a surprise. As Rose held Dave's hand, talking softly about the baby, his fingers twitched. Her heart leapt. "Dave? Can you hear me?" she asked, her voice breaking with emotion.

Very slowly, something remarkable happened. Dave's hand moved again, slightly but unmistakably. Rose gasped, tears of mixed emotions brimming in her eyes. She squeezed his hand gently, encouraging any further response, but there was no additional movement. It was a small, fleeting gesture, but to Rose, it was a glimmer of hope in the relentless darkness.

Despite this small sign, Dave remained in a coma. The doctors had been cautiously optimistic about the reflex movements but there were no significant improvements. The weight of the situation began to press heavily on Rose, each day stretching out with a sameness that was both comforting and excruciating.

Dr. Aline became a frequent visitor, not just as Dave's doctor, but also as a support for Rose. During one of her visits, he sat beside Rose, taking a more somber tone than usual. "Rose, we've reached a point where we must consider long-term plans for Dave," he said gently, his eyes sympathetic. "His condition is stable, but the lack of progress means we need to start preparing for the possibility that he may not wake up. There's a facility I recommend that specializes in the care of coma patients. They have the resources and expertise to manage his care effectively."

Rose listened, her heart sinking with each word. The thought of moving Dave, of uprooting him from the hospital that had become their second home, was daunting. "I need some time to think about this," she whispered, her voice barely audible.

"Of course," Dr. Aline replied, placing a comforting hand on Rose's shoulder. "Take all the time you need. We're not in a rush, but I needed to start this conversation now. We're here for you, Rose."

The news hit Rose hard. Later that day, while sitting alone by Dave's side, she felt the baby kick, a stark reminder of the life growing inside her. Tears streamed down her face as she placed Dave's hand on her belly, whispering, "Dave, our little girl needs you. I need you. Please come back to us."

Her pregnancy progressed, and at her next check-up, the doctor confirmed the gender of the baby. "It's a girl," the doctor smiled, showing Rose the ultrasound image. The joy of this news was tinged with sadness, as Rose wished Dave could have been there to share the moment. She bought a small pink teddy bear that day, placing it by Dave's bedside, imagining how he would have chosen the softest, cutest toy for their daughter.

As the weeks passed with no improvement in Dave's condition, Rose finally made the decision to move him to the specialized facility. It was one of the hardest decisions she had ever made, feeling like a betrayal, yet knowing it was in his best interest.

The day of the move was filled with a quiet sadness. Hospital staff who had become like family gathered to say their goodbyes to Dave, each one hugging Rose, offering words of support and encouragement. Rose held back tears as she packed up the small personal items that had accumulated around Dave's bed—photos, drawings from nieces and nephews, and the little pink teddy bear.

The journey to the new facility was somber. Rose rode in the ambulance, holding Dave's hand throughout the trip. When they arrived, the staff welcomed them warmly, but the new environment felt cold and unfamiliar. Rose set up Dave's new room with the same personal items, trying to recreate a sense of home for him.

Over the next few days, Rose visited regularly, spending hours talking to Dave, playing music, and sometimes just sitting silently, holding his hand. Each visit was a mix of hope and heartache, the reality of their situation settling around her like a heavy blanket.

# Chapter Sixteen

Rose settled into her new routine with a heavy heart. She had rented a condo close to the facility where Dave was now staying, allowing her to be near him every day. Each morning, after a night of restless sleep interrupted by dreams of a life that once was, she would wake early, prepare a small breakfast, and make her way to Dave's side by sunrise. There, surrounded by the muted beeps and soft hums of medical equipment, she spent her days.

The facility was different from the hospital; it was quieter, less hurried, but it lacked the familiar faces that had become a comforting presence during the initial months of Dave's coma. However, the staff was kind and attentive, making every effort to make Rose and Dave feel cared for.

During her visits, Rose would update Dave on the progress of their baby. She would rest his hand on her belly, hoping for a kick that might bridge the gap between him and their growing daughter. "She's quite active today, Dave," she would say softly, her voice a blend of tenderness and sorrow. "I think she's going to be just as stubborn and strong-willed as her father."

Dr. Aline continued to be a regular visitor, not just professionally as Dave's doctor, but as a support to Rose. His presence was a comfort, a stable pillar in the midst of her swirling emotions. During one visit, he brought with him a small gift—a book of classical nursery rhymes. "For the baby," he said, handing it to Rose. "It's never too early to start reading to her."

Rose took the book with a sad smile, touched by the gesture. She would read aloud from it to Dave, hoping that the familiar cadence of her voice and the rhythm of the rhymes would reach him somehow, would signal to him the life that was waiting for him outside his slumber.

As the weeks turned into months, Rose meticulously documented her pregnancy in a journal she kept in her purse. She wrote letters to Dave, describing each doctor's visit, each ultrasound, the way the seasons changed outside the window of their condo. Sometimes, she would paste pictures of the nursery she was preparing, each detail chosen with care—a soft palette of colors, a crib with gentle curves, a mobile of stars and moons that spun quietly above where their daughter would lay her head.

Despite the support and the routine she had established, the weight of her situation often found her in moments of profound loneliness. There were evenings when she returned to the condo, the silence of the empty rooms amplifying the absence of Dave's laughter, his touch, his presence. She would stand at the window, watching the sunset paint the sky in hues of orange and pink, her hand resting on her belly, feeling the kicks and stirs of their daughter as if she were reassuring her mother, "I'm here."

One particularly tough day, as Rose sat by Dave's side, the reality of their situation felt overwhelming. The doctor had just left after a routine check, his report unchanged—no progress, stable but still unresponsive. Tears welled up in her eyes as she held Dave's hand, her voice breaking as she whispered, "I miss you so much. We need you. Our little girl needs you. Please, try to come back to us."

It was during one of these visits that Rose felt a stronger than usual kick. She gasped softly, the sensation pulling a laugh from her amidst the tears. "Did you hear that, Dave? She's really making herself known today." She placed his hand on her belly again, imagining for a moment that Dave could feel their daughter's movements, that he could share in this moment of life amidst the stillness that surrounded him.

Rose's days continued in this pattern, each one a repetition of the last—visits filled with one-sided conversations, updates about a pregnancy that Dave had no visible way of knowing about, and the slow, painful reconciliation with the possibility that he might never wake up. Each day she left the facility, her glance lingered a little longer on Dave, a silent plea in her eyes for any sign of change, any hint that he might return to her and their awaiting daughter.

As the due date approached, the nursery at the condo was ready, filled with everything a baby could need, each item a testament to the hope and love of a mother fighting the shadows for her family. And each night, as Rose lay in bed, she would place her journal on her nightstand, the pages filled with words meant for Dave, a chronicle of a time marked by waiting, hope, and the unwavering strength of a woman holding onto the promise of life in the midst of uncertainty.

One afternoon, as Rose was slowly packing up her belongings from her daily visit to Dave, she felt a sharp pain in her lower abdomen. It was sudden and intense, unlike anything she had experienced so far in her pregnancy. Gripping the edge of the chair, she tried to steady herself, hoping the pain would pass. But instead, it intensified, each wave stronger and more alarming than the last.

Panicking and alone, Rose managed to call for a nurse using the emergency button in Dave's room. The nurse arrived quickly, finding Rose pale and doubled over in pain.

"We need to get you to the emergency room now," the nurse

said urgently, supporting Rose as they made their way to the hospital wing attached to the long-term care facility.

The memories of her previous miscarriage flooded back as Rose was wheeled through the long hallway, each moment heightening her fear. She couldn't bear the thought of going through that loss again, not when she had already imagined a future with her daughter, not when she had already felt the life stirring inside her so vividly.

At the emergency room, the doctors acted quickly, administering pain relief and running a series of tests to determine the cause of her pain. Ultrasound machines hummed and monitors beeped incessantly as Rose lay there, trying to focus on the doctors' assurances that they were doing everything they could.

Finally, after what seemed like an eternity, the obstetrician came with news. "The baby is okay," he began, and Rose let out a breath she didn't realize she had been holding. "However, it looks like you have a severe case of placental abruption. It's not complete, but it's serious enough to warrant immediate hospitalization and strict bed rest for the remainder of your pregnancy."

The relief Rose felt at hearing her baby was alive was tempered by the realization of what bed rest meant—she would not be able to visit Dave as regularly. The thought of not being by his side, especially when he was in such a vulnerable state, filled her with an overwhelming sadness.

Rose was moved to the maternity ward, where she was set up in a room with a window that looked out over a small garden. It was peaceful, but no amount of pleasant scenery could lift the weight from her heart. She was confined to her bed, with only her thoughts and the occasional visit from the hospital staff for company.

Dr. Aline came to visit as soon as he heard about her situation. He sat by her bed, his expression a mix of concern and professional calm. "I'll make sure Dave is looked after, Rose," he reassured her. "And I'll keep you updated on any changes. I know this isn't easy for you."

Rose nodded, her eyes brimming with tears. "Please, just tell him I love him. Tell him about the baby, about everything."

"Of course," Dr. Aline promised.

As time went on, Rose felt each moment stretch tortuously long. She was visited daily by a nurse who monitored her and the baby's health. Her mother and Sofia took turns staying with her, bringing updates from Dave, relaying the details of his care, and the songs they played for him that Rose had picked out.

They also brought recordings of Dave's room—sounds of the life-support machines, the quiet murmur of the staff, the soft background music they played in his room—anything to help Rose feel closer to him.

Rose took to writing letters to Dave, pouring her thoughts, fears, and hopes onto paper since she couldn't be there with him. She wrote about the baby, about her dreams for their future, and how she wished he could be there to share these moments. Her mother would take these letters and read them aloud to Dave during her visits, a ritual that brought them all some comfort.

The enforced separation from Dave was painful for Rose. She relied heavily on the visits from her family to bridge the gap, each update a lifeline thrown across the chasm of her current confinement. Her heart ached with the need to be by his side, to hold his hand, to speak to him about their daughter and the life they still hoped to share.

However, her priority had to be the health and safety of their unborn child. Rose clung to the hope that by following the doctors' orders, she was ensuring a future where she could bring their daughter into the world safely, a world where, hopefully, Dave would one day return to them.

As her due date approached, the reality of giving birth without Dave by her side became increasingly difficult to bear. Rose decorated the room with pictures of Dave, filled it with his favorite music, and had his shirt—the one he wore on their last day together before the accident—draped over a chair beside her bed, its fabric worn and comforting.

The days were long, but Rose counted each one.

As Rose's due date approached, a mix of excitement and anxiety filled the air. Her room was prepared with all the necessities for childbirth, each item meticulously checked and rechecked by the hospital staff. The anticipation of Lilly's arrival was overshadowed by the news that Dave's condition was deteriorating. Dr. Aline delivered the news during one of his visits, his face somber.

"Rose, I'm afraid Dave's neurological responses are weakening," Dr. Aline explained gently. "It's difficult to say what this means long-term, but it's clear that his condition is getting worse. We're doing everything we can to make him comfortable and monitor his vitals closely."

The news hit Rose hard. The thought of bringing Lilly into the world without Dave ever getting better was a reality she had feared but never fully accepted. Tears streamed down her face as she tried to process the overwhelming emotions—a mix of impending joy at the arrival of her daughter and profound sorrow for Dave.

"Thank you for telling me, Dr. Aline," Rose managed to say through her tears. "Please, just make sure he's not in any pain."

"Of course, Rose. We're all here for him, just as we are for you," Dr. Aline reassured her, squeezing her hand gently before leaving the room.

The days that followed were a blur for Rose. Her family and the hospital staff provided incredible support, ensuring she had everything she needed while keeping her informed about Dave's condition. Sofia often stayed with her at night, talking about the future and helping Rose prepare emotionally for the birth.

Then, one early morning, just a few days shy of her due date, Rose awoke to a sharp contraction. The pain was intense, signaling that Lilly was ready to make her entrance into the world. Nurses rushed into her room, quickly preparing for the delivery. Rose's mother arrived just in time, her presence a comforting constant as the labor progressed.

As Rose focused on breathing through each contraction, her thoughts drifted to Dave. She imagined him by her side, holding her hand and encouraging her. The pain of his absence was acute, but the imminent arrival of their daughter brought a renewed sense of purpose.

After hours of labor, under the careful guidance of her obstetrician and the supportive presence of her mother and Sofia, Rose gave birth to a beautiful baby girl. "Lilly," she whispered as she held her daughter for the first time. The emotional weight of the moment was overwhelming—joy, relief, and a profound sense of love filled the room.

Lilly was perfect, with a tuft of dark hair and eyes that seemed to take in the world with a curious gaze. As Rose held her, she felt a connection that transcended the pain and loss of the past months. "Your daddy would have loved to see you," Rose told Lilly, tears of joy and sadness running down her cheeks.

In the days following Lilly's birth, Rose tried to balance her time between recovering from childbirth and visiting Dave. With Lilly in her arms, she would sit by Dave's side, talking to him about their daughter, describing every detail from the way she wrinkled her nose to her peaceful sleep.

Dr. Aline continued to visit, providing updates on Dave's condition, which remained critical. The stark contrast between the new life Rose held in her arms and the life slipping away in the hospital bed beside her was a constant struggle.

Rose faced the reality of raising Lilly alone, holding onto the hope that Dave might still wake up. Each visit to Dave's room was a reminder of the dreams they had shared and the cruel twist of fate that had altered their course. Yet, Rose remained steadfast, a pillar of strength for her daughter, ensuring that Lilly knew her father through stories, pictures, and the undying love that still connected them as a family.

Through it all, Rose's resilience and the support of her loved ones provided a foundation for the new life she was building with Lilly, a life filled with love, tempered by loss, but driven by the hope of better days ahead.

Lilly was growing stronger each day, her eyes more alert and her tiny hands always reaching for something new. Despite the joy that Lilly brought into her life, Rose was acutely aware of the sorrow that lay just beneath the surface, especially when visiting Dave. His condition continued to worsen, and with each visit, the hope that he might one day wake up to meet his daughter dimmed a little more.

One afternoon, during one of their visits, Rose did something she had imagined countless times throughout her pregnancy. Carefully, she placed Lilly in Dave's arms, arranging his hands so they cradled their daughter securely. The nurses had helped, understanding the significance of this moment for Rose. Lilly lay quietly, nestled against her father, oblivious to the gravity of the moment but somehow pacified by the closeness to her dad.

Rose took a step back, her eyes filling with tears as she watched the scene before her. "Look, Dave," she whispered through her tears, "here's our beautiful daughter, Lilly. She's everything we dreamed of and more." Rose hoped that somewhere in the depths of his unreachable consciousness, Dave could feel the warmth of his daughter, that somehow this moment could transcend the barriers his condition had imposed.

That day, Rose stayed longer than usual, talking to Dave about their daily routines, describing how Lilly's smile was beginning to show and how she had begun to babble incoherently, sounds that Rose imagined were baby attempts at talking to her dad. As she spoke, Rose placed Dave's hand gently over Lilly's back, guiding him to caress their daughter. It was a bittersweet interaction, filled with love and an overwhelming sense of loss.

Rose's mother and sister, who had been her steadfast support system since the onset of this ordeal, prepared to return to Spain. Their own lives had been on hold, and as much as they wished to stay and support Rose, they needed to return to their responsibilities back home.

Their departure was emotional, laden with promises to return soon and regular updates via video calls. Rose felt a profound loneliness settle over her as she watched them go, her anchor to normalcy leaving her side. Now, it was just her and Lilly, with the weight of her situation feeling heavier than ever.

Without her family's physical presence, Rose's visits to Dave became her sole connection to her old life. She talked to Dave about everything—their family back in Spain, how Lilly's personality was beginning to shine through, and even mundane details about the weather and the little park she visited with Lilly to feel the sun on their faces.

But with each visit, Dave's physical decline became more apparent. His responses, even the minor reflexive ones, became fewer and farther between. Dr. Aline, who had been a constant source of support and medical guidance, prepared Rose for the inevitable.

"Rose," Dr. Aline began during one of his visits, his tone more somber than usual, "I need you to be prepared. Dave's condition is declining rapidly. We're seeing significant deterioration in his vital signs, and it's important that we discuss his end-of-life care."

The words hit Rose like a physical blow. She had known this conversation was coming, yet hearing it made her feel as if the ground had shifted beneath her. "I... I understand," she managed to say, her voice barely above a whisper.

"We'll do everything we can to keep him comfortable," Dr. Aline reassured her, placing a compassionate hand on her shoulder. "It's important now to think about what Dave would have wanted during this time and how we can honor those wishes."

Rose nodded, her mind reeling as she tried to process the reality of facing a future without Dave. The next days were spent in quiet contemplation and profound sorrow as she tried to reconcile her dream of a family reunited with the stark reality that Dave might never meet Lilly outside of his current state.

She continued her daily visits, now more for her than for him, telling Dave about Lilly's milestones, her first real laugh, which sounded like music to Rose's ears, and how she was learning to grasp objects, her tiny fingers curling around toys with determination.

During these visits, Rose would often read aloud from books of poetry, something Dave had always loved. She chose verses about love, about life and loss, hoping the words would comfort both Dave and herself, a soothing balm for their wounded hearts.

As the inevitable drew closer, Rose arranged for her mother and sister to be present via video call during her visits, ensuring that even from afar, they remained a part of these precious, painful moments. Together, they shared stories, reminisced about better times, and supported each other through the heartbreaking journey of saying goodbye to Dave.

Each day was a delicate balance of cherishing the moments with Lilly and grappling with the sorrow of Dave's decline. Rose's resilience was tested in ways she had never imagined, but through it all, she held onto the love that had brought her and Dave together, the love that had created Lilly, and the love that would carry her forward, no matter what the future held.

# Chapter Seventeen

As autumn gave way to the crisp beginnings of winter, the leaves falling and blanketing the earth in a myriad of colors, Rose's world inside the hospital room remained unchanged, gripped in a relentless winter of its own. Dave's condition was deteriorating rapidly, his heart struggling to maintain its rhythm, causing him to drift in and out of heart failure. Each incident was a stark reminder that the end was drawing closer, a reality Rose faced with a profound sense of helplessness and sorrow.

The medical team worked tirelessly, adjusting medications and treatments to manage Dave's condition as best they could. Dr. Aline, ever present, provided Rose with constant updates, his face often mirroring the gravity of the situation. During one particularly difficult day, as Rose sat beside Dave, holding his hand while Lilly slept quietly in her carrier beside them, Dr. Aline entered the room with a somber look.

"Rose, I'm afraid Dave's heart went into failure again early this morning," he explained gently. "We were able to stabilize him, but each episode weakens him a bit more. It's important to prepare yourself. These are signs that we are possibly approaching the end of his journey."

Rose nodded silently, her eyes fixed on Dave's pale, serene

face. The room felt unbearably quiet, the only sound being the soft beeping of the heart monitor and Lilly's gentle breathing. The reality that Dave might soon leave them was a weight so heavy, it threatened to crush her.

Later that evening, after Lilly was settled for the night in the small adjoining room the hospital had arranged for her, Rose returned to Dave's side. The hospital was quiet, a hushed sanctuary under the muted lighting. She sat there, looking at Dave, reminiscing about their life together—their first meeting, their wedding, the dreams they had shared. Now, here she sat, contemplating a future without him, a future she felt unprepared and unwilling to face alone.

In the solitude of the hospital room, Rose found herself speaking to God, her words a mix of prayer and desperation. "Lord," she whispered, her voice breaking, "if it wasn't for Lilly, I don't know if I could go on should Dave leave us. He is my heart, my life. Please, I'm begging you, don't take him away from us. But if it's his time, please give me the strength to bear it. Help me be strong for our daughter. She needs me, and I need her."

Tears streamed down her cheeks as she poured out her heart, her fears of living without Dave consuming her. Lilly, now the beacon of light in her darkest times, was the only thing that kept her tethered to life. The thought of her daughter growing up without her father was unbearable, yet Rose knew she had to find the strength to build a future for Lilly, no matter how shattered her own heart might be.

As days passed, Dave's periods of stability became fewer, and the medical interventions more frequent. Each visit to the hospital was charged with a tense anticipation, Rose bracing herself for the worst. During these visits, she would often read to Dave from their favorite books, share news of Lilly's latest antics, and play the songs that had defined important moments in their lives, all while holding his hand, cherishing the warmth that still lingered there.

One quiet morning, as the first light of dawn crept through the window, casting a soft glow over Dave's peaceful face, Rose felt a calm settle over her. It was as if, in that moment, she found a silent acceptance of the inevitable. She spoke to Dave with a tender clarity, "My love, you have fought so bravely. It's okay to rest now. We'll be okay. Lilly and I will hold you in our hearts forever."

With Lilly by her side, Rose continued to navigate the daily challenges. Her conversations with God became a nightly ritual, each prayer a plea for strength to face the days ahead and a request for peace for Dave, should his time come. She prayed for guidance on how to explain to Lilly one day about her father, how to keep his memory alive and vibrant, so that her daughter would always know how deeply she was loved by the man who had helped give her life.

The support from her family, though miles away in Spain, was a constant comfort. Video calls with her mother and Sofia were filled with tears and laughter, stories exchanged, bolstering Rose's spirits and reminding her that she was not alone in her journey. They discussed plans for the future, tentative steps toward a life that would honor Dave's memory and celebrate the life they still had to live.

Through it all, Rose held tightly to the belief that love, even in the face of overwhelming grief, could carry them through. She clung to the moments with Lilly, each smile and giggle a precious reminder that life, though forever altered, still held moments of pure joy.

As the days grew shorter and the air colder, Rose

prepared herself for what was coming. She surrounded Dave with love, filled his room with the sounds of their life together, and waited, heart heavy but steadfast, for the moment she would have to let go.

The end came on a night that seemed no different from the countless others that had preceded it, a night marked by the quiet hum of the hospital, the soft glow of the lights in Dave's room, and the vigil that Rose had maintained with a devotion that was as unwavering as it was filled with sorrow. She sat by his side, holding his hand, Lilly asleep in her carrier beside them. The room felt charged with a silent, heavy anticipation, as if the very air knew that the moment they had all been dreading was drawing near.

As the clock ticked softly in the background, marking the passage of time with a relentless regularity, Rose leaned closer to Dave, her eyes never leaving his face. The lines of pain and fatigue etched into her features were a testament to the months of watching, waiting, and praying for a miracle that she knew now would never come. Her heart was heavy with the knowledge of what was to come, the final farewell she was about to bid to the love of her life.

"Baby, you've been so strong through all of this," she whispered, her voice thick with emotion. Each word was a tremble of love and grief, a soft caress meant to bridge the chasm of silence that had settled between them since the accident. "I have prayed for you day and night, watched over you. You are my everything. You've been my hero, my rock. You've taught me strength when I was weak, been by my side through it all. I know you can't feel your pain, but I feel mine. I will show Lilly the world, make her know you and who you were. We will be okay. You can let go. I love you!"

As she spoke, a tear rolled down her cheek, landing softly on the back of Dave's hand. The room was silent, save for the gentle beep of the heart monitor and the distant sounds of activity in the hospital. Rose's words hung in the air, a tender yet heart-wrenching farewell filled with love and the pain of imminent loss.

And then, there it was—the moment that seemed to stand still, a profound stillness that enveloped the room. Dave's breathing, which had been labored, slowed even further, each breath more shallow than the last. Rose held her breath, her eyes fixed on his face, memorizing every line, every contour, as if trying to imprint his essence into her very soul.

The heart monitor's steady beep began to falter, the intervals growing longer, the sound becoming erratic. Panic and peace warred within Rose's heart as she tightened her grip on Dave's hand. She leaned in, her forehead resting gently against his, her other hand cradling his face.

"Stay with me, just a little longer," she murmured, her voice a broken whisper, though she knew it was time to let him go.

The monitor's beeping slowed, a haunting cadence that seemed to echo the breaking of her heart. Then, with a final, long beep that seemed to resonate with a finality that was both terrifying and relieving, the line on the monitor flattened.

Dave was swallowed by the darkness, his struggle ending in the quiet of the night, leaving behind the woman who loved him more than life itself and the daughter who would never know her father's embrace.

Rose sat there in silence, her body numb, the hand that had held Dave's so tightly now feeling the cold absence of his life force. It was done. Dave was gone. The love of her life, her partner, her confidant, had left her in the most final of ways. A sob broke from deep within her, shattering the oppressive silence of the room. She cried out, not just in sorrow, but in a release of all the months of pent-up fear, anxiety, and anticipatory grief.

As the initial wave of grief passed, Rose slowly lifted her head, her eyes red and swollen from tears, her face a canvas of pain and resolve. She kissed Dave's forehead gently, a final gesture of love and goodbye. "I will always love you," she whispered. "Thank you for everything."

Gathering herself, she stood up, her legs shaky but holding. She looked down at Lilly, still sleeping peacefully, oblivious to the sorrow that had just unfolded. Rose's heart ached anew at the thought of the future her daughter would face without her father. But she knew she had to be strong—for Lilly, for Dave, and for herself.

She picked up Lilly, holding her close, feeling the small warmth of her daughter's body against hers. "Your daddy loved you so much, Lilly," she said softly as she walked to the window, looking out into the night. The stars twinkled back at her, a vast tapestry of light against the darkness, a reminder of the world's immense beauty and immense cruelty.

In the days that followed, the hospital room, once filled with the silent hope of recovery,

was now emptied, the traces of Dave's presence slowly being packed away. Rose arranged for a small, intimate service to celebrate Dave's life, a tribute to the man he had been and the love they had shared. Friends and family gathered, each person carrying a piece of Dave in their hearts, sharing stories, tears, and laughter.

Rose stood with Lilly in her arms, her posture steady, her eyes clear. She spoke of Dave, of his kindness, his strength, his undying love for both of them. She promised to keep his memory alive, to tell Lilly every story, to celebrate his life through their living.

As she spoke, a sense of peace settled over her. It was not the end of her journey, but the beginning of a new chapter—one she would write with Lilly, with Dave's memory etched permanently in their hearts, guiding them, inspiring them, and reminding them of the strength of love, even in the darkest of times.

After the service, which was as beautiful as it was heartrending, Rose arranged for Dave to be cremated. It was a quiet affair, just the immediate family and a few close friends, all gathered to witness the final step in saying goodbye to a man who had touched their lives deeply. Rose held Lilly close throughout, the tiny baby a beacon of hope and continuity in the solemnity of the moment.

Once the cremation process was completed, Rose received Dave's ashes. They were handed to her in a simple, elegant urn, the cool touch of the ceramic a stark contrast to the warmth Dave had exuded in life. Holding the urn close, Rose felt a surge of resolve. She knew exactly where Dave's final resting place should be—their island home where they had shared countless dreams and built their life together.

A few days later, Rose booked a flight back to the island, a place that held so many memories, both joyous and bittersweet. As she boarded the plane with Lilly snugly strapped to her chest, Rose felt a mixture of emotions. There was fear, undoubtedly, about returning to a place so full of Dave's presence and their shared past, but there was also a profound sense of necessity. She needed to bring Dave back to the place they both loved, to the very spot on the beach that was their sanctuary, where they had spent many evenings watching the sunset and dreaming of their future.

The flight was long, and Lilly was remarkably calm throughout, gazing around with wide, curious eyes or sleeping peacefully against her mother's heartbeat. Rose looked down at her daughter, a wave of love washing over her. She whispered stories of Dave to Lilly, telling her about their island adventures, the way Dave would laugh as he chased the waves, and how he would hold Rose close under the starlit sky.

Upon arrival, the island felt both hauntingly familiar and painfully different. The lush greenery, the vibrant flowers, and the warm breeze were all as beautiful as she remembered, but now they carried a weight of solitude and remembrance. Rose took a deep breath as she stepped off the plane, Lilly in her arms, and made her way to the house that had been their paradise.

The house was just as they had left it, though now it seemed to echo with the silence of Dave's absence. Rose walked through each room slowly, reintroducing herself to the space, each corner a montage of memories flashing before her eyes. She set up Lilly's crib, filled the kitchen with groceries, and tried to imbue life back into the home that had seen so much joy.

The next day, Rose took Lilly to the beach, to the spot that had been theirs—their haven of laughter, love, and dreams. It was a beautiful part of the shoreline, where the trees whispered secrets to the ocean and the sand sparkled under the sun like a blanket of stars.

Holding Lilly in one arm, Rose opened the urn with her other hand. She stood at the edge of the water, the waves gently kissing her feet. "This was your daddy's favorite place," she told Lilly, who looked at her with innocent, trusting eyes. "He loved it here, and I know he would want to be part of this forever."

With a deep breath, Rose scattered Dave's ashes into the sea. The ashes mingled with the sand and water, carried gently by the waves, a final merging of Dave with the nature he loved so much. Rose watched as the water took him away, her heart heavy but also filled with a sense of peace. "Goodbye, my love," she whispered. "We'll always be here with you."

From that day forward, Rose and Lilly lived on the island, the place that had meant everything to their small family. Rose raised Lilly in the embrace of the lush island wilderness, surrounded by the memories of Dave. She told Lilly stories of her father every day, ensuring that though Lilly would never meet him, she would feel his presence and know his spirit.

Rose taught Lilly to love the ocean as Dave had, to explore the forests, and to see the beauty in the simple, quiet moments. They spent evenings on the beach, watching the sunset just as Rose and Dave had, talking about everything and nothing. Rose instilled in Lilly the values Dave had held dear—kindness, courage, and the endless pursuit of dreams.

As Lilly grew, so did her curiosity about her father. Rose answered her questions with honesty and love, often pulling out photographs or showing her the spots around the island that had been significant to them as a couple. Lilly's favorite was the beach where Dave's ashes had been scattered; she felt close to him there, playing in the waves, building sandcastles, and whispering her little secrets into the ocean breeze, hoping it carried her words to her father.

Rose never remarried. The love she had for Dave was eternal, and she felt him by her side in every breeze, every wave, every ray of sunshine. She lived fully, for Dave, for Lilly, and for herself, her life a testament to the enduring power of love.

# Chapter Eighteen

Several years had passed since Dave's ashes were scattered on the beach, and Lilly had grown into a curious and spirited child, her laughter and energy breathing new life into every corner of the island. Rose watched her daughter grow with a mixture of pride and nostalgia, seeing so much of Dave in Lilly's bright eyes and adventurous spirit.

One rainy afternoon, as a storm swept over the island, bringing with it the drumming patter of rain and the cleansing scent of fresh earth, Lilly decided to explore the attic—a treasure trove of memories that Rose had packed away. Amidst old photo albums and various keepsakes, Lilly found an old answering machine, a relic from a time before her birth, coated in a fine layer of dust.

Curious, Lilly carried the answering machine downstairs to the living room where Rose was curled up with a book. "Mom, what's this?" Lilly asked, her eyes wide with curiosity.

"Oh, that's an old answering machine. We used to use it to record messages from people when we weren't home to answer the phone," Rose explained, setting her book aside and smiling at the artifact of their past life.

Lilly, ever curious about gadgets and their workings, quickly found an outlet and plugged the machine in. They both watched as the small red light flickered to life, indicating there were unheard messages. Pressing the play button, Lilly's face lit up with excitement at the prospect of hearing voices from the past.

The machine crackled to life, and Rose's younger voice filled the room. "Hey guys, this is us from the past! On our way home." There was a light, playful tone in her voice that made Rose's heart swell with a mixture of joy and sadness.

She giggled slightly in the recording, nudging Dave, "Dave, say something."

Then came Dave's voice, clear and vibrant, bringing an instant silence to the room as both Rose and Lilly listened intently. "Hey future me, you're now married to the most beautiful person in the world. Treat her with love, respect, and make her your priority for life. See you soon."

The message ended, and the room fell silent, the echo of Dave's voice hanging in the air like a poignant melody. Lilly turned to look at her mother, her eyes reflective and deep. "Was that daddy?"

Rose nodded, tears glistening in her eyes as she reached out to pull Lilly into a tight embrace. "Yes, honey, that was your daddy. He loved us very much, and that message was from a very happy day for us."

Lilly snuggled closer, taking comfort in her mother's arms. "He sounds nice. I wish I could have met him."

"I wish that too," Rose whispered back, stroking Lilly's hair. "But he's always here with us, in our hearts and in the love we share. He's in the breeze, in the waves, and in the laughter we share on this island."

The answering machine, with its brief message from the

past, became Lilly's most cherished discovery. It was a tangible link to the father she never knew but felt deeply connected to through the stories and the essence of the island they called home. Rose knew that while the pain of losing Dave would never fully fade, the strength of their love—the love that created Lilly—would continue to guide and protect them.

As the storm outside began to wane, leaving fresh puddles and a sense of renewal, Rose and Lilly remained together, wrapped in a warm embrace. Outside, a rainbow stretched across the sky, a vibrant and hopeful bridge across the horizon, mirroring the unbreakable bond between them, a small family marked by loss but defined by enduring love and the legacy of a voice that would forever echo in the heartbeats of both mother and daughter.

And so, on an island of dreams, amidst the timeless dance of waves and wind, Rose and Lilly continued their journey. It was a life marked by the past but reaching always towards the future, under the vast, starry sky that once watched over two lovers and now guarded a mother and her daughter, forever bound by the sea, the stars, and the undying memory of a man who had loved them beyond measure.

JANNIK PETTERSON

# Epilogue

As Dave lies in a coma, his brain constructs an intricate reality based on sensory inputs from the real world around him, mingled with his memories and deepest subconscious. The sounds of hospital machinery, conversations between doctors and visitors, and even Rose's voice pleading with him to wake up, filter through into his coma-induced dreamscape. Each real-life stimulus transforms into a vivid, symbolic event in his internal world, leading him to believe that he is experiencing signs from Rose reaching out from beyond.

The rustling of curtains, the beeping of machines, the name of the doctor, the ring in his hands, Lilly, and soft background music—all these merge into Dave's dreams, shaping his perception of an alternate reality where Rose is communicating with him spiritually. Even though he believes these are signs from an afterlife or another realm, they are, in fact, distorted interpretations of the actual, ongoing events around his hospital bed

Printed in Great Britain
by Amazon